THE CIRCUS AFFAIR

MICHELE E. NORTHWOOD

Copyright (C) 2020 by Michele E. Northwood

Layout design and Copyright (C) 2020 by Next Chapter

Published 2020 by Magnum Opus – A Next Chapter Imprint

This book is a work of fiction. Apart from known historical figures, names, characters, places, and incidents are the product of the author's imagination. Other than actual events, locales, or persons, again the events are fictitious.

All rights reserved. No part of this book may be reproduced or transmitted in any form or by any means, electronic or mechanical, including photocopying, recording, or by any information storage and retrieval system, without the author's permission.

Dear Reader, you may have already read my memoirs, ('Fishnets in The Far East: A Dancer's Diary in Korea' and 'Fishnets and Fire-eating: A dancer's true story in Japan',) and if this is the case, you will already know that I had an extensive career in entertainment. So, I have a little quest for you whilst reading this book. Although this novel is a work of fiction, there are ten events within the story which actually happened to me. Other than the fact that I did work in a circus in Brazil and lived in a tiny caravan, can you guess the true parts of the story?

Send your suggestions to - antologiadeaguilas@gmail.com and I 'll let you know how well you did! I hope you enjoy the story, kind regards, Michele xx

*This book is dedicated to my husband, Randy.
My partner on this stage we call life.*

AN ODE TO ALL NONE BRITISH READERS

This poem is to apologise/apologize.
I do not wish to offend your eyes,
But I´m a Brit and you may think
My spelling's completely on the blink. (fritz)

My sombre/somber poem's for you to see,
You may not write the same as me.
You use a `z´ when I use `s´
In cosy/cozy and idealised/idealized. I guess

I add a `u´ when you do not,
In honour/honor and colour/color (It happens a lot!)
Ambience/ambiance and travelling/traveling
Our difference in spelling is a curious thing!

So as you manoeuvre/maneuver through this book,
And at these variances, you look,
Mistakes for you are not for me,
(It's the way that I was taught you see.)

I need to emphasise/emphasize this well...
Before you assume I cannot spell!
I hope you'll enjoy this book you've bought,
and not give these differences another thought.
Kind regards, Michele xx

PROLOGUE

"I can't believe we're doing this," Lisa shouted above the roaring engines of the aircraft as they finally set off down the runway. "Going to work in a circus, and Brazil of all places!"

She flicked her long, blonde hair back and grinned at each girl in turn, examining them with her wide, naïve eyes, waiting for similar, positive, uplifting responses.

Her enthusiasm was lost on the other three. They managed a weak smile in reply, each one thinking how young and inexperienced she appeared to be, compared to the three of them. For Melissa and Sarah, travelling abroad to work was nothing out of the ordinary. They had spent the past ten years on the road, travelling the world, working as dancers in a variety of different venues. They met up from time to time on various contracts, but this was the first time either of them had worked in a circus.

Wendy found Lisa's exuberance irksome. She looked out of the window to distance herself. Whereas Lisa was itching to get there, Wendy was much more reticent. She did not relish the thought of working in a circus. Unlike the others, she had done it before, although a long time ago. She was only doing this job because she needed a means of escape from her former life. She laughed inwardly at the cliché. She was literally running away with the circus; fleeing from a life she did not even want to think about. Her stomach was still cramped as though it was being squeezed by a giant fist, squashed in a tight knot. It was only when the plane left the runway that she felt her breath ease slightly, daring to think that, maybe, just maybe, she had finally escaped the domineering clutches of her husband.

As Lisa continued with her banal chatter, Wendy glanced in her direction again, feeling more than a little melancholic for what she considered her lost youth. *How carefree she seems,* she mused, feeling old, although, in reality, she was far from it. The past six years with her abusive husband had sucked the life out of her until she was a mere husk of her former self. *There is nothing there, she has no history. She holds no scars of past disappointment, there isn't the slightest chip on her clean slate,* she thought, with a hint of envy.

Melissa noticed Wendy emit a huge sigh on take-off but mistook it as an almost silent expletive towards Lisa's incessant chattering. She glanced across at Sarah. The redhead caught her eye, tossed her head towards the ceiling, rolled her eyes and finished with a slight shake of her head to show that she also found Lisa's exuberance a little exasperating.

Oblivious to the tick-tacking passing between the others, Lisa expounded on her childlike expectations and assumptions of circus life. The others listened, enjoying the idealised portrayal. Wendy knew that the young girl's idea of circus life and the reality would be poles apart.

"I can just imagine it now..." Lisa's eyes sparkled, and her excitement began to infected Melissa and Sarah without them even realising it.

"A beautiful Big Top which appears as if by magic overnight, in the middle of a grassy field, with twinkling fairy lights..."

Wendy laughed. "She's been reading too many Enid Blyton children's books!"

The others grinned but continued to listen.

"There'll be barrel organ music echoing out around the grounds and surrounding areas, like a beacon that forces passers-by to stop in their tracks and come towards the sound. As though they're hypnotised."

"Bloody hell!" Sarah's expletive made the others laugh out loud but still, Lisa continued.

"We'll be surrounded by performers practising in the ring all day and night to perfect their acts," she said, grinning, knowing that they were laughing at her, all be it good-heartedly. "And...there'll be sunshine every day, flowers, balloons.... oh, and popcorn," she finished with a flourish. "Lots and lots of popcorn and... we'll all live happily ever after!"

Melissa and Sarah burst into laughter at her idealistic notion.

Wendy frowned, cleared her throat and looked at the teenager. "Listen, I don't want to burst your bubble or anything but I've worked in one before, I've lived the reality."

"Really?" Lisa jumped back into her seat, folded her hands on her lap and stared attentively in Wendy's direction.

"First of all," Wendy began, "the magical Big Top has to be built up and pulled down and you will be expected to help with that. The beautiful, green, grassy field that you are imagining could be exchanged for a car-park or disused piece of wasteland covered in cowpats or dog shit. Working in the winter could find you wading almost knee-deep in mud. Be prepared to buy some wellington boots because you're going to need them. The twinkling fairy lights, along with the caravan electricity are powered by generators, so the show lights are only turned on at showtimes. These same generators are usually turned off every night at midnight – or even before if the petrol is running out or if the person whose job it is to turn them off wants to go to bed a bit earlier.

"As for your music, the days of Barrel Organ entertainment are well gone, I'm afraid. Music is usually pumped out from a CD player or computer attached to high voltage speakers. The only people it is likely to attract from afar are neighbours in the surrounding area who come to complain because they're pissed off with hearing it. And as for the dedicated circus artists, Huh! The only thing they practise is how to drink excessive amounts of beer. This usually means they end up in drunken brawls, which further evolves in them running around the site waking everyone else up in the early hours of the morning.

"Their wives or other halves are jealous, backstabbing, overprotective vixens, who guard their male partners with vigilant eyes that borders on obsession because they know that their men can't be trusted for love nor money. Even so, they're afraid that they're going to lose them to any other female, who may or may not find their partners attractive. This leads to catfights over their apparently sex-starved husbands, so be prepared for plenty of backstabbing, jealousy, and snide remarks. Well, that's how it was in my last circus anyway.

"And finally, sunshine flowers and balloons? Ha! I don't think so! Well, sun yeah, because it's Brazil but anything vaguely associated with a storybook, you might as well forget it."

"But, will there be popcorn?" Lisa's enthusiasm was visibly deflating like one of the balloons she had so enthused about a few seconds earlier.

"Oh, great! Well, thanks for that," Sarah muttered despondently. "I can't believe I've let myself be talked into doing this," she shook her head. "I'm getting too old for all this shit!"

"I can hardly wait!" Melissa mumbled, brushing her curly, black hair out of her face, her voice laced with sarcasm.

Everyone looked at Lisa, waiting for another effervescent comment. "Well, despite everything you've said, Wendy, I'm still excited. I can't help it," she replied with a grin.

The other three gave a playful groaned.

"So, what is everyone expecting to get out of this contract?" Wendy signalled the air- stewardess and asked for a Jack Daniels and coke. "Me personally, I'm not looking for anything special. I want a quiet life, free from worries. I'll work, stay in the caravan or whatever they give us to live in, and that's me done."

"Snap," Melissa replied, not wanting to disclose her embarrassing past. She had fallen head over heels for a guy who, after almost a year together, had confessed that he was married. She would love to find the perfect man and settle down, but she was scarred, humiliated, and still hurting from this man's betrayal not only to her but to his wife.

Sarah's dreams of a long term relationship had been deterred by her travelling lifestyle. She had had a few flings in the past but nothing that lasted and she had become hardened to relationship failure. Her past partners were usually too in love with their own careers to take a romantic step towards commitment. "Well I can't see any of us falling for a Brazilian," she replied. "There's the language barrier for a start…"

"Yeah, plus they'll probably all be partnered off or married anyway," Melissa added.

Lisa's eyes glazed over. She was itching to find love. Apart from a hasty fumble during the High School's graduation Dance, she had never had a boyfriend.

Sarah grunted. "Then there's their other halves, their wives, partners or long term girlfriends to worry about."

"What do you mean," Lisa asked innocently.

"Weren't you listening to what Wendy said a minute ago or is your head still in the clouds?" Sarah replied.

Lisa looked out of the aircraft window. "Actually it's above the clouds," she pointed and giggled at the nebulous coverage floating like circus candyfloss below them.

"Remember," Wendy said, "there will be men from all over the world working in the circus, they don't necessarily have to be a Brazilian. There's bound to be a lot of Latin Americans there too." As she spoke, her mind was working overtime. She had no intention of getting involved with anyone. She would, however, prefer it if they all found boyfriends and moved in with them. That way, she could have the accommodation to herself. *What could I say to them so that they'll all hook up with someone and leave me to relax in the caravan alone?*

She pondered. "You know what? I think what we need to do is make a pact."

"What do you mean?" Lisa frowned.

"We should find someone who can provide for us throughout the contract, regardless of whether we intend to stay with them afterwards or not," Wendy stated.

"Ooh! I'm not sure I'm comfortable with that," Melissa, forever the romantic, voiced. If she *did* find the perfect man, she was positive she wouldn't want the other girls crashing in his caravan. She'd want him all to herself.

"That's a good idea, Wendy. Someone who won't mind the rest of us crowding into their caravan at any time of the day or night, when we need somewhere to crash," Sarah replied, warming to the idea. She had never found anyone that she wanted to settle down with long term. She was afraid of commitment but she'd never admit it, and she wasn´t ashamed to use people to get what she wanted out of life.

"You need to target the owners of the biggest caravans," Wendy explained, conscious of the fact that she had omitted herself from her last statement by using `you´ instead of `we´. Someone with a proper shower and toilet in their caravan, which actually works, so we don't have to use the public showers because they are usually appalling!" Wendy replied.

There was a silence as they all looked across at Lisa. Her face showed her abhorrence at their statements. Her mind in turmoil.

"You've got no idea what you've let yourself in for, have you?" Wendy said with a malicious grin.

But, as it turned out, none of them did!

CHAPTER ONE

After collecting their luggage from the carousel, they stacked it onto a wonky trolley and Sarah tried to coax it towards the exit doors. Once outside, they found a tall, dark-skinned, black-haired Adonis holding up a battered piece of card with four names, each one vaguely reminiscent of their own.

"I think that's supposed to be us," Sara said, pointing in the catwalk model's direction, "Meloosa, Windy, Sana, and Liza."

The quartet broke into laughter; a mix of nervous, coquettish, flirty titters as they waved at the stunning example of the male species standing in front of them.

Adonis smiled and waved back. They stopped, watching his approach as he strode towards them. His shoulder-length hair rippling behind him as though a gentle breeze had chosen to accompany him.

He came to a stop beside Wendy and took her holdall. Sara proffered her bag for his other hand. Lisa and Melissa were left to carry their own. Adonis turned, hitched the two bags onto his shoulders and strode away, pushing the trolley as all their eyes fell to his tight buttocks.

"Oh my God!" Sarah pretended to fan herself with her free hands. "If all the men in this country look like him, I think we just might be able to pull off Wendy's pact after all!"

"Let's hope so," Lisa grinned.

They followed Adonis outside to the car park then sat in relative silence as the car left Campo de Marte airport and headed into the centre of Sao Paulo where the circus tent was situated.

As they were driven along, the girls discovered that there was a gradual progression of habitable dwellings, from the poorest of the poor to the very rich. Living virtually side by side, the slums led to crumbling old buildings covered in graffiti and adorned with washing lines of grey coloured clothing. Later, these progressed to become tall apartment blocks that dwarfed the houses below them. Eventually, these led to decent-sized abodes with private grounds, manicured gardens, and tall, high fences.

Eventually, Adonis slowed the car to a gentle stop and the girls stared at the huge white tent with raised points which rose towards the sun like peaked meringues. Thin, red stripes fell down the sides, reminding Lisa of strawberry sauce on a swirling ice-cream and she breathed a sigh of contentment.

Adonis grabbed a suitcase from the pile and with his other hand, beckoned them to follow him.

"Don't look now, but we're being watched," Sara muttered conspiratorially. The girls walked past the entrance, lugging their bags and suitcases past the box office situated off to the right. Three pairs of narrowed eyes peered at them from behind the glass windows, examining them with expressions of angry revulsion as though the dancers had crawled out of the nearest sewer.

"Bloody hell, you can literally feel the hatred emanating towards us!" Wendy said, expressing what they were all thinking.

"Yeah, I can feel it too. Why is that?" Lisa asked.

"As I said on the plane, we're competition," Wendy replied.

"Competition?" Lisa frowned. Confused, she glanced in Melissa's direction for an explanation.

"They think we are possible contenders to take their husbands away," Melissa explained.

"But they don't know the first thing about us!"

"That doesn't appear to matter," Sarah replied.

Adonis dropped the suitcase in front of the biggest trailer on the site, waved good-bye and left.

"Ah! Girls, you have arrived," a booming male voice shouted from across the field. He stood on the veranda, surrounded by hanging plants, garden furniture and an awning. He held his arms open as though he expected the girls to run into them for a hug - he would be gravely disappointed. The chances of that happening were nil. The girls came to a complete standstill and took in his jovial face, his rotund balloon-like body, and his hair scraped back into a straggly ponytail that almost reached his waist.

"What the fuck is that?" Wendy muttered as they stood like startled sheep, huddling together for comfort.

Lisa stifled a giggle.

"Look around you, we appear to be on display," Sarah said. She turned her head slowly from left to right at the weird conglomeration of humans that were slowly emerging from their caravans or opening windows to get a better view.

"Has time stood still or what?" Melissa replied as the members of the circus who happened to have seen them had come to a complete standstill. They stood gawping as though the dancers had just stepped out of an alien spaceship.

"Curtains are twitching all around us too, look," Lisa replied.

The girls, without realising it, were returning the curious looks of bewilderment as they witnessed the circus folk now going about their daily routines. As Wendy had stated, there was nothing circus-like about these people. In fact, apart from the lines of caravans behind the tent reminding them all where they were, they could have been anywhere. There were no painted clown faces or artists in lycra leotards practising acrobatic routines. These were ordinary people doing ordinary things: hanging out washing, sitting in fold-up chairs smoking, reading the newspaper or enjoying the sunshine.

The rotund guy, with the straggly long hair who appeared to be the boss, dropped his arms and resorted to beckoning them towards him. They shuffled forwards, feeling more than a little uncomfortable knowing that all eyes were on them; they were centre stage as they tried to maintain equilibrium and juggle their abundance of bags and suitcases. The boss adopted a hands-on-hips position, his legs open and his head held high.

"He's either the boss or considers himself to be some sort of superhero," Melissa whispered as the girls approached.

"Superman," Wendy sang as they reached their destination with sniggers etched across their faces.

"Hello!" their host oozed confidence. "My name is Edwaldo. Welcome to my circus. Circus Felicidade. Come, come." He climbed the two steps to the terrace of his large caravan and turned to face the girls. "Put your bags here. Come inside."

The quartet entered a huge, immaculately clean trailer. A large open kitchen/living room area with a wall of mirrored wardrobes met their eyes. Plush sofas positioned at strategic angles, a display cabinet and various pieces of art completed the interior design. Edwaldo approached a large wooden desk by the door. It was covered in piles of papers, receipts, circus posters, tickets, and a host of stationery products which looked as though someone had inverted a pen holder and emptied it all over the desk.

Edwaldo plonked himself into his old office chair that groaned under his weight and leaned precariously to the left. He eyed the group like a farmer who had just bought four heifers. They stood before him – due to the absence of chairs- feeling exceedingly uncomfortable.

"So, my four dancers from England!" (He pronounced it `In-ger-land.') Welcome to Circo Felicidade!" he said again, waving his arms as though he was directing an orchestra.

Melissa quickly looked around, she was waiting for a group of strolling musicians to appear from the other rooms and serenade them or, at least, an explosion of music to burst through the caravan speakers. Nothing happened and the whole thing seemed rather lacking. A total anti-climax.

Seeing that the girls were unimpressed by his exultant display of enthusiasm for their arrival, Edwaldo picked up his mobile, gabbled something in Portuguese and then sat back grinning at the girls again. "Now you meet my wife. She is the single trapeze star of our show and also the choreographer."

No sooner had he spoken than a tall, slim woman with striking, long, blonde hair strolled into the caravan.

"Ah! Mi Amor!" Edwaldo grinned at his wife but a reciprocal welcome was not forthcoming. "Girls, this is my wife, Sienna," he told them.

Sienna refrained from looking in her husband's direction. She gave the girls a weak smile; a greeting which did not quite reach her eyes. She folded her arms across her ample chest with one hand resting on her chin as though she was doing an impression of the 'think' emoticon. Then she looked at the girls from head to toe, assessing them with an openly contentious manner. "Here we work two shows a day, four shows at the weekends. I will take you to your caravan. I warn you. This is not a big van, but enough for you."

At her scathing remark, the girls glance furtively at each other.

"Come, come!" Sienna bustled them out of the caravan and wafted her fingers towards the luggage. "Bring your bags." She sauntered seductively down the two caravan steps – a movement spoilt by the bright yellow clogs that adorned her feet - and strode towards the amalgam of caravans, trailers, and converted vehicles which constituted the circus artists' homes.

The girls picked up their belongings and followed after her. Juggling bags, suitcases and holdalls they broke into an occasional skip or run to try and keep up with Sienna's long legs.

Moments later, the five came to a stop outside a caravan which was approximately 14 feet long. The once-white painted trailer was a peeling hunk of splotches and rust stains. One small window in the middle of the van was held together by two large strips of masking tape. The front door had a hole drilled through it which held a sturdy length of chain. This ran through a second hole drilled into the wall and fastened together with a thick padlock. The tiny lock below the rickety handle had not been sufficient for the previous inhabitants.

"Bloody hell!" Wendy exclaimed. "What did they keep in here? A wild animal?"

"You stay here," Sienna announced.

"You don't say!" Wendy's sarcasm was lost on Sienna who fumbled with the padlock and opened the creaking door with such care the girls were sure it was about to snap off the hinges.

Sienna stood back for them to peer inside the gloomy interior.

"Home sweet home!" Sarah said sarcastically.

Lisa refrained from comment and scrunched her nose up in disgust.

"I will leave you to organise. Tomorrow, at ten o'clock you start rehearsals. Come to the foyer tent." Sienna turned and walked away.

Melissa peered inside again. "How the hell are four of us supposed to live in this rabbit hutch of a caravan? There isn't room to sling a bloody cat!"

"Or a rabbit," Wendy quipped.

"And it smells," Lisa added.

Two double beds at either end of the caravan made up with the cushions and bolsters that could convert both beds into seating. A tiny kitchen ran down the middle of the van and opposite was a slim wardrobe with an even tinier bathroom beside it.

"Well, girls, it doesn't like we'll be given anything else so we might as well make the most of it." Melissa clambered inside and put her bags on the nearest bed.

Lisa joined her, then fingered one of two curtains that hung at the edge of the two beds. She pulled it across and back again. "Why would anyone want curtains pulled across their bed?"

"For a bit of privacy," Melissa explained.

Lisa frowned, "How do you mean?"

"Well, imagine if you brought a boyfriend back, you wouldn't want everyone watching what you were doing, would you?"

"No..." Lisa replied, "but even if I pulled the curtain, they'd still hear me wouldn't they?"

Wendy laughed. "Yeah, and feel the caravan moving! What's that sign they usually put on vans...? 'If this caravan should start a rocking, please don't come knocking,' or something like that."

The others laughed.

"I don't think we should have any amorous encounters in here, there just isn't any room!" Sarah said.

"Deal!" Wendy replied. She looked across at the other two who nodded in assent.

"May I make another suggestion?" Sarah asked. "Can we also agree to turn our mobiles off at night so they won't disturb other people who want to sleep? On my last contract, it drove me crazy and I don't want another six months like that."

"But, what if there's an emergency? People need to be able to get in touch with us," Lisa replied.

"Well, let's compromise. Everyone must put their phone on vibrate, that way it shouldn't be too annoying," Melissa suggested.

"Okay," Sarah agreed. The others nodded.

They looked around at the dirty caravan and their dumped luggage and sighed.

"So, what's next?" Lisa put her hand on the tiny kitchen worktop and then pulling it away, she screwed up her nose in disgust.

"This has to be the smallest accommodation I've ever had the displeasure of having to live in!" Wendy sniffed.

"It smells like an animal has crawled up and died in here. This is the pits!" Lisa replied.

"Okay, well., let's try and be positive," Melissa said with an air of authority. "Obviously, the first thing we need to do is clean it. Once we've done that, it will feel better, and we can make it feel homelier with a few of our photos and things dotted about."

"But, where the hell are we going to put all the bloody suitcases?" Sara asked.

"Yeah, and all the clothes inside the suitcases?" Lisa added.

Wendy stood up. "Caravans are deceptive little units. It's surprising how much stuff you can manage to hide away under the seats and inside the cupboards."

The other three cast dubious glances at each other and at what would be their home for the next six months.

"It will eventually feel like home," Wendy added, "honestly."

"Home sweet home." Lisa's sarcastic tone was not lost on the other three.

"Our own little rust bucket!" Sarah said, equally sarcastically.

∽

By the end of their first day, the four girls sat at both ends of the caravan. Melissa and Lisa on the bed by the door, Wendy and Sarah on the other, admiring their accomplishment. The entire trailer had been scrubbed inside and out, articles of clothing and personal belongings had been crammed into the overhead cupboards, tiny wardrobe, and equally tiny bathroom. New bed linen adorned the two makeshift beds and an oscillating fan took pride of place on the kitchen units, trying its best to waft slivers of cool air in the girls' direction. The suitcases had been stored in the 'belly box'- a metal container purposely built under the van for storage. It was strategically placed next to another box which was also under the caravan. Wendy had explained to her rapt audience that this was a tank to collect any waste from the bathroom toilet and shower. If the circus camped on 'hard ground', for example, a car-park, then they would need to use it. In a field, holes would be dug to conveniently catch all bodily functions.

"This is a nightmare!" Sarah complained as they sat drinking wine out of four mismatched drinking receptacles they had found in the cupboards. "We'll end up killing each other if we have to live in these close conditions for the remainder of the contract."

"I feel the need to keep the door and windows open all the time," Lisa admitted. "When we are all in here, it feels so claustrophobic."

"Here, here!" Wendy confirmed. "Now do you all understand what I meant when I said that you each need to find a man who will not only let you stay in their caravan but will let the rest of us crash there too."

"Someone with a good-sized trailer," Lisa added, making a mental note.

"Yeah, a good size trailer with hot water so we don't have to keep boiling pans full of water like we've been doing all bloody day," Melissa said.

"Someone who can afford to take us out to eat and get us away from the show for once in a while," Sarah replied.

"Challenge accepted?" Wendy asked raising her glass towards the centre of the caravan.

"Accepted," the three girls replied. They all clinked glasses, each deep in thought and each with varying levels of enthusiasm.

∼

The following morning, dressed in black jazz-boots and an assortment of lycra leggings, leotards, or matching two-piece ensembles in various colours, the girls began rehearsals.

Sienna had commandeered the ring and plonked an aged CD player on the ringside stalls, a wooden walkway, painted red that ran around the outside of the sawdust strewn ring separating the audience from the artists. It stood about a metre high and sort of resembled benching. It was normally used by the artists during the show to stand on, run around on, or sit on during the various acts. Now, Sienna was using it as a substitute table.

She gathered the girls together and attempted to teach them the opening routine – a marching number with drums - which basically consisted of them marching around the ring in different formations for two and a half minutes and banging a drum that was held in place by a thick strap that was slung over their shoulders.

"Thank God nobody from home will be coming to watch us," Wendy whispered after a while.

"Why's that?" Lisa replied.

"Because this choreography is a pile of shit!"

The others tried to smother their giggles as Sienna stood a few feet away, fiddling with the sound on the CD player.

As the morning wore on, and they were completely sick of marching, word spread quicker than a viral video on social media that there were four foreigners in the ring. The entire circus seemed to find some reason or another to enter the tent and saunter through at a snail's pace in order to get a good view of the newcomers. The male members eyed the girls lasciviously, whereas the women assessed them through biased, critical eyes; weighing them up as future competition in the search for (or the keeping of) a man.

At lunchtime, Sienna clapped her hands, gave them an hour to eat, and left with her CD player. The girls slumped onto the ringside, looking disillusioned by the whole affair. Sweat was pouring off them, more from the heat within the tent rather than the exertion that would usually cause them to perspire.

"I don't really understand why the show would go to all the trouble of bringing English dancers if they didn't want us to do any real dancing," Sarah began. "I mean, it's perfectly obvious that Sienna is not a real choreographer. We could all dance her into the ground."

"Yeah, it all seems a bit weird, doesn't it?" Wendy agreed. "I was told that we were going to dance at the Metropolitan Theatre in Rio de Janeiro; we can't work in such a huge, prestigious venue like that with crappy routines like these!"

"Let's go and get some lunch before we have to be back here again!" Melissa replied.

The girls wandered across the field; the rays of the bright

Brazilian sun burning down on their uncovered backs, augmenting their irritation, hunger, and plight as they headed back to the tiny caravan.

∽

Four days later, Sienna deemed them ready for the show and the final rehearsal had taken place. This was when they had discovered exactly why the routines were amateurish and so easy. Naively believing that they were to be the only dancers in the show, they were momentarily stunned when in sauntered an amalgam of wives, girlfriends, and offspring of the male artists. They were all shapes, sizes, and ages. Flotsam, with little or no dance training whatsoever. The four Brits stood out like supermodels in a holiday camp beauty competition.

Sienna unsubtly repositioned the motley group around the four new arrivals, and by the end of the afternoon, the tension was rising to boiling point. Those who had considered themselves to be the best of the worst had now been relegated to second position. Their usurping from centre stage did not go down too well. The quartet listened to their disgruntled mutterings in Brazilian or Latin American Spanish. Although they didn't understand their incensed angry chuntering, the girls could easily deduce that the long-standing members of the ballet were far from happy. That and the flashes of hatred in the other women's eyes made the newcomers feel more like outcasts than ever before. The quartet realised that their estancia in Brazil was not going to be easy.

CHAPTER TWO

A WEEK later the girls were already disillusioned by the mundanity of the show routines. The huge, corrugated metal haulage container, which was used as the dressing-room, was where they spent most of their time during the shows. It was a confined space, so full of pent up frustration, mistrust, and misplaced anger at the new arrivals that the girls dreaded entering it. The existing group had shuffled apart to make space for the quartet to sit at a long plank of plywood that ran the length of the container. It was used as a makeup table, with strategically place mirrors dotted along the wall. A string of lightbulbs liberally drooped around the same wall provided them with enough light to apply their make-up. There was an aged fan placed at one end of the container. The oscillation had ceased to work many moons ago so only three women, the oldest of the group, were the advantageous trio who received a slight benefit from its weak attempt at circulating the hot air that filled the room. The mishmash of women had purposely separated each girl from the other three, supposedly to make them feel more insecure than they already were. Their resentment of the girls made the atmosphere within the room seem charged with electricity as though one tiny spark would cause the dressing-room to explode with a barrage of abuse and fighting.

Sienna had only augmented the situation by announcing that the show destined for the Metropolitan theatre needed to be of a much higher quality than the poor effort presently being performed in the circus tent. She informed them that a new choreographer was going to be brought in and all new routines would have to be learned.

"Edwaldo wants to do a magic act of the calibre of David Copperfield. Huge illusions with lions and white tigers, disappearing elephants, and a host of other tricks," she informed all the members in the dressing-room.

"David Copperfield the magician or David Copperfield by Charles Dickens?" Melissa sniggered, but the comparison was lost on the other three.

As the Latinos stirred with renewed interest at Sienna's announcement, their enthusiasm was soon dampened by her next comment.

"The English girls will be the principal assistants and do most of the main tricks," she said, singling out the four girls with a flick of an accusatory finger. "But you will all be involved in some way or another."

The Spanish chuntering and clicking of tongues made it perfectly clear how they all felt.

∽

After a week on-site, the girls had made no progress whatsoever in the prospective boyfriend department. The four of them were still squashed together in the cosy caravan despite being ogled from afar on numerous occasions by various male members of the cast.

One evening, Melissa stood backstage looking around absently at the hive of activity going on around her. The flying trapeze stood in their white lycra costumes speckled with sequins. On their feet were various coloured clogs. They doused their hands with resin and then wrapped thin, white straps of material around their wrists to aid in their catching. They were so engrossed in their activities they spoke to each other in lowered tones without making eye contact with anyone.

Miguel, the juggler stood to one side religiously practising his seven ring trick over and over again. The lion trainer walked up and down in front of the metal tunnel, constantly checking its rigidity and making sure there was no possible escape for the big cats. Benjamín, the Ringmaster stood near the curtains with his cue cards in one hand and a microphone in the other. He glanced towards Melissa and smiled. Melissa, startled, shyly smiled back. She was surprised and slightly unnerved when he maintained eye contact. A frisson of excitement ran down her spine. Over the past week, since they had begun to work in the show, the artists had kept themselves to themselves. A few had nodded curtly at the girls but no one had attempted a conversation. The girls felt this was a mixture of contempt at their usurping of the females' positions in the ring, or they assumed that the lack of a common, shared language could also be a reason for the males' aloofness.

Melissa unconsciously ran her hands down her opening costume in order to look away from the piercing dark eyes of Benjamín. She loved his opening costume of knee-high black boots over tight, cream trousers. A long, black, open coat brushed around his ankles. It was delicately embroidered with swirls of silver stitching and adorned with silver braiding on the cuffs, epaulets, and front. He had long, straight, jet-black hair that hung loose down to his waist. His slightly crooked, pointed nose gave his face character. He reminded Mellissa of a modern-day Vampire mixed with a fairy tale prince charming. She risked a glance upwards again. His gaze remained on her. He threw back his hair with one sweeping hand movement and sauntered towards her.

"Hola, soy Benjamín," he grinned, "¿cómo te vas?"

Melissa realised that he was speaking Spanish, not Portuguese.

She silently thanked God that she had paid attention in her high-school Spanish classes and could converse a little.

"Hola, yo soy Melissa," she replied.

"¡Vaya! Hablas Español!" Benjamín grinned.

Melissa translated his sentence in her head before replying. (Wow! You speak Spanish.)

"A little," she replied holding up her index finger and thumb to portray the tiny amount of Spanish she could remember.

"Better in English?" Benjamín questioned. Melissa breathed a sigh of relief.

"Yes, please!" She glanced towards Wendy, Sara, and Lisa who were stood together watching her interaction and grinning inanely.

"I like how you dance," Benjamín continued.

"Thank you," Melissa replied, feeling a blush of embarrassment creeping up her neck. Not only for his attention but also for being reminded of the pathetic dance moves she was being forced to perform.

"You dance…er…how you say… very elegant."

Melissa resisted the urge to correct his adjective for an adverb. "Thank-you. I like the way you dance to the music during the acts," she replied.

He looked surprised that she had watched him. "Tonight I have a party in my caravan. You want to come?"

"Can I bring my friends?"

"Yes, of course. Er…ten thirty, okay?"

"Yeah, great!"

Benjamín sauntered back toward the curtains as the first bars of music rang out from the small orchestra signalling the beginning of the show.

"What was that all about?" Sarah asked as Melissa wandered back over to them. "What did he say?"

"He's having a party tonight, and we're all invited." The three girls prickled with excitement.

"Excellent!" Lisa exclaimed. "Maybe this way, we'll actually get to talk to some guys rather than be ignored all the bloody time!"

"Come on, Melissa said, hoisting the strap for the cumbersome drum onto her shoulder and picking up the drumsticks. We've two shows to get through first!"

∼

By the time the girls arrived at Benjamín's huge trailer, the party was in full swing. Latin American music blared out of two speakers, which were balanced precariously between the open window and the thin outer layer of the caravan's insulation. A large, foldable table stood in front of the caravan on the left-hand side. It was laden with an amalgam of multi-coloured bowls and dishes holding an array of different food. On the right, was a smaller table with enough bottles of spirits to open a small bar. There was a 50-litre keg of beer, and columns of plastic cups leaned against the caravan in regimental fashion, just waiting to be used.

"Shit, I think we were supposed to bring food or at least a bottle," Sarah mumbled. "We look like we're gate-crashing!"

"Well, if we'd been given more than a few hours' notice, we could have prepared something or bought some booze," Wendy sighed as Benjamín spotted them and wandered over.

"We didn't know we had to bring food," Melissa voiced in apologetic tones. She stared into his eyes and swooned.

"No problem. You can bring for next party," he grinned, looking only at her. "Come, come, have a drink, dance, have fun!" He put his hand on the small of Melissa's back and walked her towards the drinks table.

"Come on girls, follow me," Sarah linked arms with the other two and they followed Melissa into the crowd and towards the alcohol.

A few minutes later, drinks in hand, the four girls stood together surveying the scene. The partygoers were mainly men but a few younger females were dotted about.

"I've come to the conclusion that the younger male artists have brought their partners or girlfriends, but most of the older ones have left their wives at home." Melissa deduced.

"Yeah, they're probably looking after the children, but how they could possibly sleep with all this noise is beyond me," Wendy replied.

"Surely they can't all be married or partnered off," Lisa sniffed. "There must be some of them who are single."

"You hope," Sarah grinned. "Come to think of it, so do I!"

They laughed.

"Melissa's alright. She's bagged herself the star of the show!" Wendy said with a grin.

"I don't think so," Melissa looked at the ground to hide her embarrassment. "I've hardly spoken to him."

"He invited you to his party didn't he?" Lisa pointed out. "That's because he wanted you here."

"Maybe, but I feel mega nervous, I don't know why." Melissa gave her bottom lip a nervous bite.

"Don't worry so much," Wendy intervened. "A bit of alcohol always loosens people's inhibitions. You'll be fine!"

"Yeah," Sarah agreed, "And I saw the way he was looking at you during the shows. I'm pretty sure he's already smitten."

Melissa blushed, "Do you really think so?"

"Well, we'll see tonight, won't we!"

Lisa felt a pull on her elbow and turned around.

"¿Bailas conmigo?"

Standing before her was a teen about her age. She was not aware of his name, but she had secretly watched him from afar. He was her height, with blond hair tied back in a ponytail that reached his shoulder blades. He was muscular and strong with a lascivious gleam in his eyes. He grinned seductively.

"Er...what?" Lisa muttered.

"He wants you to dance with him," Melissa explained.

Lisa passed her glass to Wendy.

"Okay," she took his proffered arm and sauntered into the crowd.

Wendy glanced across at Sarah, "Well, that just leaves you and me."

"And me," Melissa replied. Sarah brushed her away with her hand. "You are already accounted for. Benjamín hasn't taken his eyes off you since you arrived!"

Melissa snuck a glance in his direction, he stood with one foot poised on the seat of a chair, his long hair falling across his shoulders. He saw her watching him and raised his drink in salutation. Melissa repeated the action. Benjamín smiled and beckoned her to join him. She found herself wandering away from the girls as though in a trance. There was something hypnotic about him that she felt impelled to be by his side. Her emotions were in turmoil, the more sensible side of her conscience was screaming to stay away. *What was she doing? She was in another country and this was a foreigner. Did she really want to become involved with someone who probably only wanted her for the duration of the season? What if she fell for him in a big way? Would she want to spend her life travelling from circus to circus and never returning home to England?*

Her more frivolous side was counter-attacking, urging her forward, telling her to take a chance. She had never felt such a strong connection towards another man and she was slightly afraid. *Go for it. What's the harm? You're entitled to a bit of fun. Who cares whether it lasts or not!*

"Hello beautiful," Benjamín grinned. "Come, let's walk."

Melissa felt the frizzle of attraction as his hand landed on her lower back making her tingle with pleasure. They sauntered together away from the party, across the encampment and down to a small stream which ran the length of the field.

∽

The following morning, Melissa and Lisa woke up to find that Wendy was sleeping in the other bed, but Sarah was nowhere to be seen. As they discussed in lowered tones the possibility that she had stayed out all night, Wendy stirred.

"Never mind Sarah. What happened with you and Benjamin?" Wendy prolonged his name with a hint of sarcastic humour in her voice as she looked at Melissa with an expectant twinkle in her eyes.

Melissa was momentarily taken aback. "Nothing really."

"Ah, come on, spill the beans! I'm dying here!"

"Well, he took me down to the lake..."

"Yeah, and?"

"Well, we were talking - he knows some English so it was easier than I had expected."

"Yeah, and, did he ask you out?" Lisa interrupted.

"Not exactly, but he did kiss me," Melissa explained.

"Ha!" Wendy pump fisted and jumped into the air. "Nice one. Brilliant, other than Edwaldo, Benjamín's is the biggest trailer on site. This is what I'm talking about," Wendy grinned with anticipation. "Very soon you'll all be able to crash in his caravan, cook in there, hell, we can virtually live in there...it'll be fabulous!"

"Anything would be better than staying in this grotty old caravan!" Lisa commented.

Melissa smiled thinly. Somehow she could not imagine Benjamín wanting her to bring the rest of her motley crew each time she was asked over to his trailer.

"Anyway, that's enough about you, Melissa," Wendy said, casting a beady eye in Lisa's direction. "Where exactly did *you* wander off to?"

Lisa dropped her eyes towards the caravan floor. "I don't know what you mean."

"Yeah, you do, young lady," Wendy gave her a sly smile. "Sarah and I saw you slinking off with that blonde guy behind the caravans."

"I..."

"Come on, spill the beans," Wendy almost sang, "What's his name? What does he do?"

Lisa wrung her hands in discomfort. "Well, he's called Mario. He does the single trapeze with his sister, but he wants to work on the high wire."

"Yeah, go on…" Wendy coaxed. "So, how old is he? Has he asked you out? And more importantly, has he got his own trailer?"

"I don't know. I think he still lives with his parents; he's only just eighteen."

"Uh oh! That's a no go. You agreed to find a man with a trailer, a big trailer to incorporate the rest of us!"

Lisa looked crestfallen. "I know, but I like him a lot!"

"What about you?" Melissa interrupted, determined to move the spotlight across to Wendy. "Where's your conquest for the evening? Lisa's may not quite fit the bill, but at least she tried. Where's your Prince Charming?"

"Well, I er… didn't find anyone I liked," Wendy muttered, not relishing being in the spotlight.

"Well, might I suggest you look a bit harder," Melissa replied, "There's plenty of time before the end of the contract."

"What's happened to Sarah?" Lisa asked, addressing the white elephant in the room.

"She hooked up with one of the flying trapeze guys," Wendy said through a yawn.

Lisa's mouth dropped open in shock. "Not with my Mario!"

"Don't get your knickers in a twist," Wendy replied with a distinct note of contention in her voice. "I said flying trapeze, not single trapeze."

Lisa visually relaxed and got out of bed. "Cup of tea anybody?"

"Coffee for me thanks," Wendy replied. "The tea here is shit!"

"Well, 'there's an awful lot of coffee in Brazil´,'" Lisa sang as she filled the metal pan with bottled water.

"Coffee for me too, please," Melissa also exited the bed and walked the two paces towards Lisa and the tiny kitchen area. "I'll make some toast."

"And I'll stay exactly where I am," Wendy slouched back on the bed. "You know what they say, 'two's company, three's a crowd', besides, there isn't room for all of us."

The girls were halfway through breakfast when the door opened and Sarah peered inside.

"Oh, you're up," she said sheepishly, preferring to look at the caravan floor rather than their faces.

"Yeah, we are," Melissa replied. "How about you? Have you been to bed yet, or are you just coming home?"

"Oh, she's been to bed, she just hasn't been to sleep!" Wendy quipped.

Sarah clambered inside and walked to the far end of the caravan. She plonked herself on the bed and lay down next to Wendy with her hands clasped behind her head, looking at the grubby paint-flaked ceiling.

"Well?" Lisa prompted.

"Well, what?"

"What happened?"

When Sarah remained silent, Lisa tossed her head in mild annoyance. "Listen, I've had to answer Wendy's questions about last night. Now the tables have turned. Come on, start talking."

Sarah propped herself up on one elbow and sighed. "Alright, alright! If you must know, I was asked to dance by one of the flying trapeze groups. His name is Fernando and..."

"Can you hear the drums, Fernando..." Lisa broke into song. Melissa and Wendy joined in. Wendy from her recumbent position on the bed, and the other two singing and dancing around the enclosed space clutching a butter knife and a teaspoon as microphones as they continued with the breakfast.

Sarah rolled her eyes. "Do you want to hear about this or not?"

"Yeah, yeah, sorry!" Lisa stopped dancing then looked at the other two and giggled.

When decorum had returned, Sarah pointed an accusatory finger in Melissa and Lisa's direction. "When you two sauntered off last night, Wendy and I were stood together having a drink when Fernando walked over and asked me if I wanted to dance."

"Quite a few other couples were dancing by that point," Wendy said, adding a little ambiance to the storyline.

"Anyway..." Sarah glanced in Wendy's direction and narrowed her eyes. An expression which told Wendy, in no uncertain terms, to shut up. "We started to dance..."

"Was it a slow dance?" Melissa asked.

"No... will you let me finish! Anyway, we got talking, as you do, and he said that his family is looking for another woman..."

"For a gangbang!" Lisa quipped.

"NO! He said that they are looking for another girl to learn the trapeze and he thought that with my hair colouring and size, I'd be perfect for the job." She grinned, looking rather pleased with herself as she saw their surprised expressions. "In fact, they want me to go for a try out this morning."

"Really? And are you going to do it?" Melissa asked.

"Why not? I've got nothing to lose. Hell, I might even get adopted by the whole family, then I won't even have to bloody cook in this 'tin can' we call home, they'll probably feed me every day too!"

There was silence for a few seconds while the news was digested.

"Bloody hell!" Wendy vociferated. "It looks like you're in the lead in regards to the bet."

"Not necessarily," Lisa replied. "She might do the trial run and be total crap."

"Thanks a lot, I love you too!" Sarah replied.

"Okay, so the jury is out until after the try-out," Melissa stated. "Can we come and watch?"

"Don't you dare! I'll be nervous enough as it is!"

"You had better have some breakfast first. You'll need all your strength to get through this." Melissa handed her the first two slices of toast, but Sarah didn´t take it.

"My head is still swimming from all the alcohol I drank last night. If I eat anything, I'll be liable to throw up with all that swinging backwards and forwards." She put her hands over her mouth. "In fact, just the thought of it is making me want to heave!"

As she ran from the caravan, Melissa picked up the kettle. "Coffee, she needs some good strong coffee."

Wendy flopped back onto her bed. "And I need some sleep!"

∼

"How did it go?" Wendy asked as soon as Sarah appeared at the caravan. The girls were sitting on a blanket on the grass, propped up with cushions. They were sipping soft drinks, reading books or writing letters as music blurted out of the open caravan door from a small stereo that Wendy had brought with her.

"Not bad, but it's so much harder than you imagine. I mean, they make it look so bloody easy, but I'm aching all over. My stomach feels like a brick, the backs of my knees are on fire from rubbing on the bar and my hands look like I've been brought up in a workhouse all my life." She thrust them out for the girls to examine. Still lightly covered in resin, her hands showed the raw callouses and red patches she had amassed during the two-hour session. "I'm absolutely exhausted!" She flopped dramatically onto the blanket, rolled onto her back and looked up at the clear blue sky. "It was a fantastic experience though!"

"But, what did they say? Do they want you to continue?" Lisa put down her writing materials to give Sarah her full attention.

Sara grinned despite her discomfort, "Yeah!"

"Excellent!" Melissa replied.

"What about Fernando, did he speak to you?" Lisa quizzed, her enthusiasm beginning to infect the others.

Sarah smiled. "Yes, of course, but it was a bit awkward because, obviously, everyone was watching me. But he managed to ask me to meet him tonight after the show."

Wendy sniggered.

"What's so funny?" Sarah asked, taking offence and getting defensive.

"I'm just imagining you. I can see you marrying him and spending the rest of your life swinging on the trapeze and travelling around the world in his trailer for the rest of your life!"

The others giggled.

Sarah picked up a cushion and threw it at her. "Yeah, right!"

Lisa stopped laughing abruptly and redness spread upwards from her neck to her cheeks as she stared ahead. The girls followed her gaze and saw Mario sauntering towards her, his hands in his pockets and his blonde hair flowing around his shoulders in the gentle breeze.

"Boyfriend alert!" Wendy smirked as Mario approached and nodded to them all.

"Hello, Lisa," he smiled. He only had eyes for her. "Can I talk to you?"

"Sure," she said and remained seated.

There was an awkward silence. Mario swayed from side to side waiting for her to stand up, but Lisa didn't pick up on his expectations.

Melissa rolled her eyes heavenwards in exasperation. She elbowed Lisa and inclined her head. "Take him somewhere else. Someplace where you can talk!"

Realising the wisdom in Melissa's words, Lisa jumped up. "Oh, yeah, right."

Mario smiled, and as they walked away he took her hand. The others watched and smiled.

"Ah! Young love," Wendy said sarcastically.

"So, we're just waiting for you," Sarah replied.

"Waiting for what?"

"You're letting the side down. You've got to find someone. We made a pact!"

Wendy stopped grinning. "I think you're all doing pretty well on your own without me. "

"That wasn't the deal," Sarah replied.

Wendy grinned, "Why do you think I suggested the bet in the first place? There was method in my madness. I knew that if the three of you found boyfriends, I could virtually have this rust bucket we lovingly call home all to myself!"

"You crafty cow!" Melissa grinned and shook her head in mock consternation.

Wendy refrained from replying. She was not ready to telling them the real reason that she was not on the look-out for a man.

CHAPTER THREE

As Lisa walked away from the girls and fell in step beside Mario, she jumped when he grabbed her hand with an abruptness that appeared almost frantic. Lisa was reminded of a drowning man reaching out, grasping at her for salvation. She smiled. It was nice to feel wanted. She felt the roughness of his palm in hers and the hard callous mounds, evidence of the hard labour involved in circus life and the many hours of training on the trapeze. She cast a shy glance in his direction. His piercing blue eyes sparkled, reminding her of glistening seawater reflected by the sun. His blond hair made him appear more Nordic than Argentinian and she found him so attractive that she couldn't believe he had picked her out. As they crossed the site, the only incommodious aspect during their intimate walk together was his tendency to wave and called out greetings to everyone they passed. Lisa hung her head, allowing her hair to fall over her face to hide her embarrassment. Everyone seemed to stop whatever they were doing to watch them walk by. She wondered if she was a passing fling, merely another conquest he was aiming towards or if she was his first, and that was the reason everyone was watching them with interest.

"We will go to the town centre, okay?"

Lisa looked into his eyes and smiled. She liked the idea of being told what to do, and she liked the feeling of belonging to someone. "Okay."

They came to a stop outside one of the larger trailers. Mario opened the door and shouted into the van, "Mamá, vamos al centro. ¿Necesitas algo?" (We're off to town. Do you need anything?)

Lisa heard a mumbled reply then the caravan shook from side to side, creaking and groaning as an obese woman waddled to the front door. She came to a surprised halt when she spied Lisa, but her folds of excess skin continued to undulate into a final resting place – something that Lisa found more than a little unnerving.

"Y ésta quién es?" (And who's this?) The woman held onto both sides of the doorframe and wheezed, staring with a critical eye at the young girl before her.

"Hello," Lisa said with a faltering smile as she wondered whether Mario's mother was holding on to the door frame to stop herself from falling over or just to try and catch her breath.

When María didn't reply and the pregnant pause seemed interminable, Mario spoke.

"Lisa, this is my mother, Maria. Many years ago, she was a very famous single trapeze artist in my country, Argentina. One day, she fell. Now she cannot work in the ring."

Looking at the obese woman, Lisa found the story hard to believe. She shook her head to rid herself of the vision of Mario's mother with her excess weight trying to swing on the trapeze and the entire structure falling into the ring as soon as her weight left the floor.

"Hello," Lisa repeated, holding out her hand.

Maria ignored the proffered hand. Reaching into her apron pocket, she pulled out a fistful of notes and offered them to Mario.

"Espera," she said as the youngsters turned to go. She reached back inside her apron and handed him a handwritten list. "La lista de compras."

"Shopping list!" Lisa grinned at Maria, trying for the third time to be amicable. Once again, she was disappointed. She received a hard, condescending glare in return. Lisa's grin disappeared from her face quicker than a fart in a fan factory.

"Come on, Lisa," Mario put his hand on her shoulder. As they walked away, Lisa could hear the caravan creak under the bulk of the huge woman waddling back to her original position.

∼

Melissa and Sarah wandered over to the tent to prepare for the first show. It was a habit they both had in common. Unlike Wendy and Lisa, they liked to be well prepared for the performances and not running around in a frantic state after leaving everything until the last minute. Sarah's trapeze lesson was later than usual that morning, and Melissa had decided to work out at the same time. When they had finished setting their costumes, they wandered into the ring in rehearsal gear. The trapeze was already in position. Melissa saw Benjamín helping them secure the huge net in place, then he picked up a hammer and went over to check one of the seating areas. She surmised that he must also be the chief handyman, as he always seemed to be pottering around doing little jobs here and there.

Seeing the girls' enter the ring, Fernando sprinted across towards them.

"Running with his clogs on," Melissa whispered, "that's got to be a feat he's spent years perfecting."

Sarah grinned and looked at him. He flashed Sarah an excited smile. "Are you ready?"

"Ready as I'll ever be, yeah, let's go." She smiled briefly in Melissa's direction before walking away. Fernando trotted beside her chatting with animated excitement.

Melissa watched them go. Fernando's attraction toward Sarah was obvious. He wore his heart on his leotard sleeve and anyone who cared to look couldn't fail to miss it. In contrast, Sarah walked with a rigidity that portrayed how guarded she was towards the whole affair.

Melissa sat on the floor opened her legs into a 'V', and stretched her arms above her head. Leaning over her left leg, she stretched her body as far forward as possible. Only a few seconds into her workout, she heard his voice:

"Hello!" The baritone voice that never failed to send shivers down her spine came from behind her. She bolted upright and, for a few seconds, she froze. Then, she brought her legs together, feeling that sitting with her legs wide open was only inviting trouble. Slowly she swivelled her body around to face Benjamín.

"Hola!" she smiled.

"What are you doing?"

"I'm limbering up, er...exercising."

"You are...how do you say? Supple."

"Thanks," Melissa twisted a few strands of stray hair around her finger.

"So, I was thinking, why are you not learning the flying trapeze? You don't want to try?"

Melissa felt it futile to explain why Sarah was up there and not her. "I prefer to keep my feet firmly on the ground, thank you very much!"

Benjamín laughed. "So you don't want to learn to do the web?"

"The what?"

"The web!" he pointed towards a single, thick rope that hung suspended from the cupola, the very top of the tent, like a dead snake.

Melissa followed the rope upwards until she saw a small loop dangling downwards three-quarters of the way up.

Benjamín followed her gaze. "That is for your hand – or even your foot when you get more advanced. It can be very elegant to work on the web and also gives you a great work out. It's probably more effective than your exercises on the floor."

Melissa's gaze went from the rope to Benjamín and back again. "Yes, maybe, but I would need someone to teach me." She bit her lip and wondered what on earth had possessed her to say such a thing!

"I can do that!"

"Are you sure? Do you have time? You always seem so busy fixing things."

Benjamín grinned, flicked his hair behind his shoulders, and grabbed hold of the rope. "I'll always make time for you. Come here."

Melissa felt herself redden at his words, but she stepped towards him and took hold of the rope.

"You must put your hands like this," Benjamín stood behind her, pressing his body into her back. Melissa fought the urge to fall into him, rest her body next to his and nuzzle his neck before turning around and kissing him with abandon. She mentally reprimanded herself for her stupidity and tried to concentrate on what he was saying.

He placed one of her hands above the other on the rope. "And now you climb the rope."

Melissa looked towards the top of the tent. I seemed so high up and precarious from her standing position in the ring. She swallowed. Her lack of spittle, due to her nervousness, caused her to cough. She was briefly reminded of her gym classes at middle school where she had always managed to get to the top of the rope but was always eager to scuttle back down again. She was having serious second thoughts, but looking at Benjamín's expectant smile, she acquiesced.

"Hala, vete!" Go on, he said, making shooing motions with his hands. "Climb."

Melissa clutched the rope as though her life depended on it and lifted her feet off the ground. As the thick cord began to swing and turn slowly giving her a panoramic view of the circus Big Top, she hoisted her legs upwards. Clamping her feet one on top of the other around the rope she pushed down with her legs and began to climb.

"That's it, keep going," Benjamín encouraged as Melissa fought the urge to scramble back down to the bottom. "Keep going, nearly there, nearly there!"

The tiny noose was just above her, but the thought of letting go of the rope with one hand and inserting it inside the loop was a daunting prospect.

"Okay, now, put your right hand into the loop and pull the cord tight around your wrist."

Melissa nodded, petrified that if she spoke, her voice would come out in a squeak, she was so nervous. Silently praying, *Please don't let me fall, please don't let me fall,* she placed her hand in the loop and tightened the strap as her legs took the weight of her body.

"Now, reach down with your other hand and grab the rope so that your arms are wide apart. Like this..."

"What?" Melissa's voice quivered and highlighted her confusion as she played for time.

"Like this..., look." Benjamín opened his arms above his head in the shape of a wide `V`.

Melissa swallowed deeply and ran her hand along the rope. *Please don't let me fall, please don't let me fall,* she continued her silent mantra as she inched her hand into position.

"Good, good, now, let go of the rope with your feet." He made it sound like the most natural thing in the world, but Melissa was far from convinced. She squinted downwards and stared at him as though he had lost his mind.

"I beg your pardon?"

"Push on the rope and let your feet go free. Simple! Like this!" He sauntered over to one of the king-poles (the main supports that held the tent up). Grabbing hold of it with both hands, he lifted both legs off the floor, "You see?"

"Huh, simple!" Melissa muttered to herself, wondering how he had managed to coax her up there in the first place. Tentatively, she released her feet and felt her entire bodyweight fall onto her strapped wrist. She hung there feeling like a flaccid piece of celery that had been left out overnight. There was nothing poetically beautiful about her blundering attempt at circus artistry.

"And now I will spin you," Benjamín said enthusiastically.

"Wait!" she yelled, "you'll do what?"

Benjamín grabbed the rope and began to turn it. Slowly at first but increasing with each revolution.

Melissa felt as though she was caught on a skipping rope as her stomach turned over and over and threatened to reproduce her breakfast. As the quickness gradually increased with each revolution and the skipping rope turned into the spin cycle on the washing machine, Melissa found her voice.

"STOP! NO MORE! STOP!" she shouted down to Benjamín. '*Please make it stop,*' her inner voice yelled.

Benjamín jolted the rope to a wavering stop and Melissa flopped from one ungainly position to another, like a rag doll on a washing line on a windy day.

"Okay, that is enough for today. Come down!"

As her eyes came back into focus and the tent came swimming past her at a gentler pace, Melissa hoisted her legs back onto the rope, carefully took her arm out of the strap and braced herself for the climb down. She glanced down at the stage floor and then wished she hadn't. It looked so far away. She felt like a kitten up a tree, she'd got up there, but did not relish the thought of having to make her way back down. Muscles in her arms that she never knew existed were crying out with red hot pain. Her legs were clamped around the rope, squeezed together as if she needed the toilet, frozen in position.

"Come down!" Benjamín repeated with the slightest hint of exasperation in his tone.

"Yeah, yeah, just give me a minute!" she called down, annoyance evident in her voice. *Come on, Melissa, you can do this,* she told herself.

It was at that point she realised that the entire flying trapeze group had come to a standstill. The flyers were stood on their board, like a flock of perched birds peering down at this fledgling who had yet to find her wings. She spied Sarah watching her with a bemused grin on her face which spurred Melissa into action.

"I'm coming, I'm coming," she shouted. Edging her way back down the rope she muttered, "Never again, never again, never again!"

Benjamín's firm grasp of her waist helped her down the last few feet, then he spun her around to face him. "Well done, well done. For the first time, that was okay," he said, casually leaving his hands on her waist. "Tomorrow, we go again," he grinned.

"Okay," Melissa heard herself say, then clenched her fists, angry at her lovesick stupidity. Would she put herself in any ridiculous situation to spend time with him? Why was she so incapable of saying no?

From up high on the board, Sarah stood completely at ease despite the altitude and the precariousness of the apparatus she stood on. Trying not to laugh out loud at Melissa's ludicrous attempt at the web she gave her a thumbs up.

"Why you smile?" Fernando inquired.

Sarah pointed in Melissa's direction. "It's her. She's hilarious! She's seriously falling for this guy, but she doesn't even know it."

Fernando looked confused. "But, she didn't fall…?"

"Never mind, Fernando," Sarah waved him away with a flick of her hand. "Okay, what do you want me to do next?"

"We'll practise the layout again, okay?" He grabbed the bar hook and threw it over the trapeze bar to bring it towards them.

Sarah stood with her legs apart, one hand on the trapeze and the other on the scaffolding. She watched the catcher, Arturo, thrusting his legs out and upwards towards the cupola to gain the correct momentum, then he dropped back so that the backs of his knees were resting on the bar. He wrapped his ankles around the trapeze ropes and clapped his hands.

"Hup!"

Sarah took a deep breath, let go of the support, and jumped off the plinth swinging towards him. She swung backwards towards the board and then forwards again towards Arturo. Letting go of the trapeze bar, she stretched out for his hands and her gut contracted violently, as she realised that her timing was off. She was falling. As she plummeted towards the net quickly followed by a barrage of Spanish expletives from Arturo, someone on the ground yanked her upwards by pulling on the safety harness she was obliged to wear.

After dangling in mid-air feeling exposed for the failure she was, she felt herself being lowered gently into the net.

Fernando looked down and cupped his hands around his mouth, "Sarah, does this mean you are falling for me?"

Sarah cringed, wondering how her sense of embarrassment could have augmented even further than it had already.

CHAPTER FOUR

Three weeks into the contract and the girls had settled into the regular daily routine. It was the weekend and they still found them tough. Performing four shows a day under the Big Top in the Brazilian heat was exhausting.

That Sunday morning, as they sat outside on a blanket eating breakfast, Edwaldo came lolloping towards them with a lopsided grin pasted across his sweaty face.

"So, girls, tonight you will do your first `pulldown´, are you prepared?"

Lisa took a bite of toast and stared at him in bewilderment. "What's a pulldown?"

"Tonight, we take the tent down and we move to the next town. Didn't you read the notice in the back of the tent?"

"Sorry, we don't understand Portuguese," Lisa answered.

"It was written in Spanish," Wendy whispered.

"Okay, so I'll tell you what to do. Immediately after the show, you need to change into your old clothes and come and find Sienna. She will give you jobs to do."

What jobs, exactly?" Sarah eyed him with suspicion, not liking where this conversation was going.

"Everyone helps in the pulldown." His vague answer left three of the girls more puzzled than before. "When it is finished, you can go back to the caravan and wait. A driver will come to take you to the next town."

The girls squinted towards him, crinkling up their noses and shielding their eyes from the sun. Edwaldo was not sure how to interpret their expressions. Despite being in authority and in a more domineering position considering that they sat on the floor below him, they had somehow managed to unnerve him.

Edwaldo dropped his gaze and glanced at the food on the blanket before lifting his head again. "Okay!" he said with forced joviality. "Enjoy!" He waddled away and the girls watched him go. They were temporarily lost for words.

"What's that supposed to mean?" Sarah asked scathingly. "Enjoy what? Our breakfast or the pulldown?"

"Definitely the breakfast," Wendy replied with a knowing nod of her head. She knew what was coming. The others were in for a huge shock.

"Exactly what jobs is he expecting us to do?" Lisa asked what they were all thinking.

"I've no idea," Melissa replied.

"It never said anything about dismantling a tent in our contract," Lisa sniffed. "I mean; do I look like a labourer or what!"

"I guess we'll find out tonight. He said he's going to allocate us different jobs to do." Sarah buttered herself another piece of toast. "I suppose we'll just have to wait and see."

"And where are we supposed to get old clothes from? I haven't brought anything to work on a building site!" Lisa continued, expressing her disgust out loud.

Wendy sniffed. "We'll just have to play it by ear tonight and then for the next time, we'll be better prepared," she said, trying to sound more positive than she actually felt.

After the fourth show finished around ten o'clock that night, the dressing-room emptied in record time. The girls, oblivious to the urgency involved in a pulldown, gathered up their belongings and stepped out into a hive of activity which took them by surprise.

All cast and crew had donned overalls and thick gloves. A resounding clanking of metal upon metal reverberated around the site as the tiered seating was being dismantled with the help of hammers. Everyone worked diligently. They all had their set jobs and executed them with a rapidity which reminded Melissa of worker ants. They picked up their loads and hoisted them back to the waiting lorries and returned empty-handed to repeat the process. Shouts of camaraderie rang out as the men shouted and joked with one another. Emotive heavy rock music blared from the aged speakers, unconsciously filling the circus employees with the incentive to work hard, and fast.

Wendy, who had seen it all before, picked up her pace and carried on walking to the caravan. The others came to a standstill, taking in the atmosphere, not quite believing what they were seeing. As they stood and stared, Sienna appeared in front of them.

"Come on, come on, get a move on. You can't just stand there. First of all, turn around and go back into the dressing-room. It is now your job to pile up all the chairs and carry them to the lorry over there." She pointed to one of the many lorries which now had long ramps leading up from the floor to the open back doors."

The girls watched as other circus performers sprinted up the ramps with a variety of objects. Sienna monitored their vexed expressions, wondering why they were immobile and not jumping to her orders.

"Come with me!" She set off walking back to the dressing-room assuming they would follow her. "Once you have done the chairs, then I want you to pack the mirrors separately and put them inside the wardrobes on the floor." She flicked her wrist to dismiss her next statement. "Leave the lights, the guys will do the lights."

When the girls remained standing there looking at her as though she was speaking Klingon, she clapped her hands. "Hurry up. I want you back here in five minutes. Chop, chop!"

Back at the Caravan, Wendy changed into the oldest clothes she could find and wondered what was taking the girls so long. It seemed like such a long time ago that she had done her last pulldown that she had completely forgotten to pack down the caravan. All the cupboard door handles needed to be tied with string to stop the contents falling out. Anything that wasn't fastened down needed to be put in a secure position for the journey. The hose-pipe and electric cable needed to be wound up and brought inside. The gas bottle needed to be disconnected and also housed in the van. She kicked herself for her stupidity. They should have been doing these little jobs throughout the day so they would be ready to leave at a moments notice. It was too late now.

Knowing that time was of the essence, Wendy left the caravan and went in search of the girls. She found them in the tent standing in front of Sienna like jittery army recruits on their first day of training. "Ah, Wendy, help the girls fold up the chairs in the ringside area and take them to the lorry over there."

While Wendy set about doing the task immediately, the others stood there looking slightly lost and overwhelmed.

"Er...The thing is, we haven't had the chance to get changed yet," Sarah replied.

Sienna threw her arms up towards the cupola and sighed. "I know this is your first pulldown, but you need to be much more prepared, much quicker. Do you understand me?" When the girls gave her weak nods in reply, her voice rose two octaves. "Well, go on then. Hurry up!"

Unsure if she meant they should hurry to their caravan or hurry up with the chairs they continued to stand there with vacant expressions pasted across their faces.

"Go, to your caravan. Hurry up! Go, go, go!" Sienna shouted.

The girls scuttled off towards their van.

"Bloody hell!" Lisa said as they ran across the field. "What have we let ourselves in for?"

"A night of hell," Sarah replied. "Just think, when they get the tent down – and God knows how long that is going to take - we then have to drive to the next town."

"According to Philipe the clown, it usually takes them about an hour and a half to take it down," Melissa informed them as they struggled into shorts and t-shirts. "But that's because they are a well-oiled team. They've been dismantling the tent for a long time now. In the beginning, he said it took them almost four hours. I guess they must have been as clueless as we are now!" Melissa giggled.

The other two were not amused.

"The next town is about a two-hour drive from here," Sarah informed them. "So, I reckon we'll be lucky to get to bed by four o'clock in the morning!" She plonked herself on her bed and gave a dejected sigh.

As the other two mumbled various expletives to show their dislike of the situation, there was a sudden pounding on the door.

"Come on, get out!" Sienna yelled.

Melissa opened the door and flashed her boss a sheepish smile. "We're coming."

"Do you have gloves?" Sienna enquired.

"Er... well, no."

"I didn't think so. Here." She handed each girl a pair of rubber, washing up gloves in a variety of colours. "These will do for today. Next week you can buy something more appropriate."

The girls donned the gloves and followed Sienna into the throng of frenzied activity as she tutted and shook her head in total disbelief at their complete ineptitude.

They reached the ringside area and Sienna ushered them over towards a forty-something-year-old woman, who was bellowing orders at any females within her view.

As Sienna spoke briefly to the woman, Wendy sidled over to join her friends.

"Girls, this is Martina," Sienna explained. "She is in charge of all the girls in the pulldown. You must do what she says, okay?"

The girls nodded absently, feeling totally at a loss with this alien-like situation. Sienna acknowledging their assent turned away and sauntered back towards her trailer.

Martina garbled something to them in Portuguese, then realised that the four new recruits had no idea what she was talking about, she broke into pidgin English. "Continue with chairs. Take chairs to lorry." The girls stood there almost in a state of shock and stared at the remaining chairs that ran around the ring, contemplating how they were going to carry out her order. Unfortunately, all Martina registered was their lack of movement and none acquiescence. Their lack of urgency prompted Martina to jump-start their inertia. "MOVE!"

The girls flinched. Jolted into action, they began to stack the chairs in piles of four.

Martina put her hands on her hips and nodded. "When you finish, find me for next job!" Then she marched away to bellow at another girl.

"Bloody hell, I don't remember reading in the contract that we had signed up for hard labour!" Sarah complained. "I feel like a prisoner doing hard time."

"Yeah, and I reckon Martina could quite easily give anyone a hard time with a voice like that," Melissa replied. "Talk about harsh!"

"Shit!" Lisa looked down at her hands. "I've already put a hole in these gloves, they aren't going to last two minutes."

Sarah pulled hers off and rammed them into her pockets, "I can't work with these silly things on. I'm better off without them!"

Lisa picked up a stack of four chairs and struggling to find her equilibrium, staggered off towards the lorry. "Come on," she urged. "I don't want to receive another earful from sergeant major Martina."

The others giggled at Lisa's seriousness, picked up some chairs and followed her to the lorry.

Ten minutes later, Martina was back. "Hurry, hurry!" she snapped as they carried the remaining stacks of ringside seating.

Picking up the pace, they waddled towards the van for the final time.

"Now, follow me."

The girls walked with her around the outside of the tent until they found two women in the process of folding up the outer side pieces of the Big Top.

"These are the `wallings´," Martina said, pointing at various piles of heavy, almost rigid, fabric, made from waterproofed hemp. Each piece had been unhooked and dropped in a heap on the ground at strategic points just around the outside of the Big Top. "Each section has to be folded in a specific way. Watch carefully how these two do it," she said, pointing to two older women who stood waiting to give the girls a demonstration.

"Bloody hell, I feel like I'm back in primary school and on some sort of detention!" Lisa whispered.

"Detention would be much easier than this!" Sarah sniffed. "Give me one-hundred lines any day!"

The two women opened the walling out into a completely flat piece. They folded it in half by standing at either side of the plastic sheeting, picking up one corner and dragging it towards the adjoining corner which was still on the ground. This was folded once again and then rolled up into a tight sausage shape. Once finished, they moved onto the next one.

Melissa looked back and saw some of the other men picking up the already folded pieces, throwing them over their shoulders and heading towards another lorry. As she marvelled at their camaraderie and synchronised efficiency, Martina snapped her fingers in front of Melissa's face.

"Pay attention!" she bellowed. "Move!"

Melissa realised that the two original women had been split up and given two girls each to teach. She had been partnered with Lisa.

"When you have finished, come and find me for the next job!"

Martina snapped and marched away to oversee the rest of the pulldown.

As the night progressed, the girls ran around, getting in a flap in this foreign environment, following Martina's barked instructions and mimicking the other girls. As the cupola and king poles – the final parts of the Big Top - were dismantled and loaded onto trucks with the help of two forklift trucks, the girls were under the wrong impression that they had finished. Martina called all the women in her extensive team together and presented them with plastic bin bags.

"Now what?" Melissa muttered. She looked down at the refuse bag and back to Martina for some sort of clarification.

As the rest of the girly crew scattered in all directions like ants disturbed in their nest, the quartet realised that their final job was to wander around the site and pick up every single scrap of rubbish they could find.

"She's got to be joking, right?" Lisa said, in a complete state of shock. "Am I seriously expected to pick up everyone else's shit that they've thrown on the ground?"

"Er, yep!" Sarah confirmed. "The girl who was folding the wallings with me said that the circus can be heavily fine if they don't leave the site how they found it."

"Well, I just don't get it," Lisa complained.

"What's not to get?"

"In all the books I've read, people usually run away to join the circus."

"Yeah, and?" Sarah asked.

"Well, surely after what we've had to do this evening, it stands to reason that it should be the other way around. I'm surprised they're not all running away in droves!"

They all laughed at Lisa's unconscious, comedic ability.

"Apparently not," Sarah replied.

"It's in their blood," Melissa explained. "I think those that are born into it just love it. They don't know any other life. This is their norm."

"Bloody hell!" Lisa moaned. "Well, don't fall in love with a circus guy unless you envisage doing this for the rest of your life!" Her sombre words left all four of them deep in thought.

Like a shepherdess calling her dogs, Martina's caustic yelling brought all the circus females to her side once again. She gabbled on in Portuguese, and when the others began to take off their gloves and disperse in all directions towards their caravans, the girls realised that the pulldown was finally over.

Martina looked at the girls and pointed in the general direction of the trailers. "Go to your caravan and wait to be taken to the next town."

"Yes, sergeant major, straightaway sergeant major!" Lisa muttered as they walked away.

"I wonder how long we'll have to wait?" Melissa thought aloud.

Wendy shrugged. "I've no idea. There's obviously not enough vehicles to pull all the caravans at once. But tonight, that's a good thing because we are going to need the extra time. We've got to pack down the caravan now."

"What the hell does that mean?" Lisa's anger was rising by the minute.

Wendy quickly explained what was involved as the others shook their head in abject disbelief.

"This is going to be a *lo...ng* night!" Sarah said. They entered the caravan and plonked themselves despondently on the beds. As each girl took a minute's respite, there was a harsh knocking on the open door.

"Hello, I am Alfonso. We go now. I drive your caravan," a tall, middle-aged man informed them.

"Okay, great," Melissa said, grabbing her bag. The girls did the same. Wendy was the most reticent. As they exited the rust bucket, they found their escort standing with his hands on his hips, slowly shaking his head with an expression of sheer incredibility etched across his face.

"You are not prepared!"

"What are you talking about?" Melissa frowned.

"Look!" He pointed at several vehicles in turn.

"What are we supposed to be looking at?" Sarah snapped. She stood with her hands on her hips, instantly taking the defensive.

Melissa and Lisa shrugged in reply while Wendy wished the ground would swallow her up as everything came rushing back to her in a flash.

Alfonso walked to the back of the caravan. "THESE!" he said in exasperation. "First, you must lift the back legs of the caravan." He walked over to point at the offending legs with an accusatory finger and looked with irritation in the girls' direction.

"I'll lift my leg in a minute and kick him in the bleeding arse!" Sarah replied. "I've just about had enough of all this!"

"This looks too complicated for me," Lisa said, shaking her head. "I'm a dancer, not a bloody car mechanic!" She bent almost double and stared at the metal legs. "Huh! Go figure. I've never even noticed them before!"

Alfonso frowned and strode to the front of their van. "Then you need to turn this handle."

"What handle?" Melissa frowned.

"Alfonso ignored her. "Then you can raise or drop the jockey wheel until the front of the caravan is high enough to drop onto the tow bar."

"The what wheel?" Sarah asked.

"Then you put on the break."

"Eh?" Lisa exhaled loudly, slowly losing her patience with the whole situation.

Alfonso shook his head at their ineptitude. "Now I take different caravan. You prepare. I come back for you later."

"How much later?" Sarah inquired.

"Three, maybe four hours, depends," Alfonso replied as he searched the belly box for the appropriate tool. "Here, use this for the legs." He pushed a cranking handle into Melissa's hands and then strode towards another trailer.

Melissa stared at the tool wondering exactly what she was supposed to do with it.

"Well, this is just great!" Sarah complained. The four of them looked from the wrench to the caravan legs and each other in bewilderment.

"In my last circus contract, I lived in an old fashioned wagon, almost like a gypsy caravan," Wendy explained, "only much bigger and separated into five different accommodation sections. I didn't have to wind up legs, I don't even think it had any."

"Oh, well, let's see if we can do it," Melissa pulled her shoulders back, sighed in determination and headed towards the caravan.

They managed to lift the two back legs but before they could walk around to the front of the van, the entire trailer tipped backwards leaving the front half of the caravan standing high in the air and the other end of the caravan shell touching the ground. At the same time, there was the distinct sound of movement from within the trailer as everything which wasn't tied down (so, basically everything), came sliding towards the back end of the trailer.

They stood looking at the home they had managed to wreck in two minutes flat.

"Shit we've broken it!" Lisa said.

Sarah cocked her head to one side and viewed their caravan now standing on a diagonal. "Bloody hell! It's standing at such a weird angle it looked like some sort of freaky modern art exhibition."

Hearing the distinct sound of laughter behind them, they turned to find Benjamín and Mario standing behind them.

"We thought you might need some help," Benjamín strode forward and took the tool from Melissa's hand.

Mario put his hands on either side of the door frame and peeped inside the van out of curiosity. "You haven't packed down?"

"NO!" The girls shouted in unison.

"I haven't got a clue what you're even talking about!" Lisa snapped.

The guys pulled the van back to its original position, lowered the jockey wheel, repositioned the back legs, and took the girls back inside their home.

"All the weight in the caravan needs to go to this end," Benjamín explained, pointing in the direction of Sarah and Wendy's bed, the nearest to the jockey wheel. "All the cupboards need tying with string so that nothing falls out. Everything must be packed down."

"Right, and who thought to pack any string in their suitcases? Because I certainly didn't!" Sarah's sarcastic comment was not lost on the rest of them.

"I've got some sticky-tape," Melissa replied. "We'll have to make do with that."

When everything was secure, the girls had calmed down and the guys had prepared the caravan, Benjamín turned to Melissa.

"I'd better get going. See you in the next town." He leaned in and planted a kiss on her lips.

Melissa was surprised and embarrassed at the same time. Her insides had stirred at his touch yet she felt strangely uncomfortable knowing that her friends were watching with interest.

Not wanting to be left out, Mario grabbed hold of Lisa's arm and copied Benjamín's actions. Lisa blushed. She was more embarrassed by the open show of affection than Melissa.

The guys patted each other on the backs and walked away.

The girls stood looking at their temporary home, wondering what the hell they were supposed to do for the next few hours.

"We'd better not sit in the caravan again or the bloody thing might tip up again," Wendy said.

"We'll have to sit out here and wait. There's nothing else for it." Melissa reached into the caravan and grabbed a blanket from the bed. Shaking it out, they dropped onto it and fell into silence.

After a while, Wendy spoke. "God, I wish we had some wine! I could do with a drink right now."

"You and me both!" Sarah replied.

"We can go and get some," Lisa said, brightening up. "There's that little shop on the corner that seems to be open 24 hours a day. We've got plenty of time. Let's go get some! It's not like we have to drive."

Sarah jumped up. "Come on then, let's go."

CHAPTER FIVE

Alfonso and the girls arrived at the new site at four o'clock in the morning. After struggling in the dark to lower the caravan legs, secure the front wheel, unravel electricity cables and hosepipes, they dumped the empty gas bottle outside the door and fell exhausted into their beds.

Two hours later, they were awoken by the sound of a fist banging loudly on their door and the shrill shouting of Martina.

"Get up, come on, get up!"

The girls struggled to open their eyes, looked at each other and frowned.

Melissa dragged herself out of bed and opened the door, squinting into the harsh, early morning sunlight that invaded her retinas and left her temporarily blind.

"Time to move," Martina informed them.

"Move?" Melissa looked past Martina and became aware of the scene playing out in front of her. The entire circus - or so it seemed - was up, out of their trailers, and working right in front of her. She spied Benjamín, Mario, and Fernando laughing together as they shouldered sections of the tiered seating structures into the already erected tent. The wallings were still to be put up, and some of the other girls were carrying the ringside boards into the Big Top. A portable stereo was balanced precariously on a stepladder spewing out more rock songs to animate the workers. The camaraderie so early in the morning only made Melissa frown. How could they be so jovial? She heard Wendy in the back of the caravan groan.

"Oh, shit! The build-up..."

Melissa turned to Martina. "Sorry, what?"

"Get up! Now it's the build-up," Martina's tone implied that she could not believe they were still sleeping. "I expect you to be in the tent in five minutes."

As she marched away, the others groaned.

Lisa rubbed the sleep from her eyes and looked at the others. "Build up? What the hell's she going on about?"

"Build up, Lisa," Wendy replied with a deep sigh, "means that we're about to do the complete opposite of what we did just a few hours ago."

Lisa's mouth dropped open in shock. "You've got to be joking!"

"I'll expect you to be in the tent in five minutes," Wendy mimicked Martina perfectly. "Well, what she expects and what is going to happen are two completely different things: First of all, I need a coffee."

"We haven't connected the gas bottle and we need to go shopping first. We're out of water." Sarah pulled on last night's clothes and looked at the girls, her tiredness and depression were mirrored in the three faces in front of her.

Wendy broke the silence by pushing past Sarah. "Well, at least let me have a bloody wee first, for God's sake!" She stomped the two steps into the tiny bathroom and banged the door.

Lisa sighed. "How long do you think it's going to take?"

"As long as I bloody well need!" Wendy shouted from the bathroom.

"I meant the build-up!" Lisa shouted back.

"God only knows," Melissa replied, then broke into a nervous giggle.

"Come on, I suppose we'd better get this over with," Sarah replied.

"Wait for me, wait for me," Wendy scrambled out of the bathroom pulling up her shorts. "Okay girls, let's go!" She jumped out of the caravan and landed with her legs apart. She thrust her fisted arm forwards. "Once more unto the breach!" she bellowed and strode with comic determination towards the Big Top with her arm still outstretched.

"God for Harry, England, and Saint George!" Melissa replied, marching behind her.

Lisa frowned and looked at Sarah who had also begun to march. "Who's, Harry?"

Sarah grinned and shook her head. "Never mind, Lisa, it's Shakespeare."

Lisa broke into a run to catch her up. "But... I thought his name was William?"

Sarah broke out laughing. "It is, Lisa, it is! Come on, let's get this over with."

∽

A couple of hours later, when Martina had declared the build-up finished and had excused them all, the girls meandered around the outside of the tent, appreciating the sun's warmth on their dirty skin. Complaining about their lack of food and their extreme thirstiness they witnessed the illusive Sienna emerging from her trailer like a chrysalis from its cocoon. Stretching her arms above her head and squinting into the bright sunshine, she smoothed down her outfit and swanned down the steps.

"Just look at her," Wendy remarked. "She thinks she's the circus equivalent of Paris Hilton."

Sienna's long, blond hair freshly washed and dried blew feather-like in the light breeze. Her freshly ironed attire greatly contrasted with the four mud-laden, exhausted, hungry, and thirsty girls before her.

"She's like the bloody queen looking down on all her subjects," Sarah muttered in disgust as Sienna threw a designer bag over her shoulder, pulled designer sunglasses over her eyes, and headed off in the general direction of what she assumed was the town centre.

"How come she hasn't done the build-up?" Lisa questioned, pouting her lip and sulking. "That's not fair."

"Because, Lisa, she's married to the owner. This is what I've been saying all along," Wendy replied. "You need to find men with the most power. Men with the biggest trailers and men who can hopefully get us out of doing shit like this. If not, it's going to be a long, hard contract!"

Sarah grinned, "I suppose by men, you mean one man. One that has got all of the aforementioned attributes, no?"

Wendy nodded as Lisa sighed and snuck a glance in Mario's direction. He was sitting on the grass, drinking beer with some of the other men. He held up his beer can with one hand and called her over with the other.

"Alright, Wendy, I get your drift," Lisa said. "But at the moment, I'm gagging for a drink, we've got nothing in the caravan, and Mario's offering me a free beer so, see ya, suckers!" she ran over to his side.

Sarah came to a standstill. "You know what? She's right." She tucked her muddy gloves into the back of her shorts and sauntered over to the men.

Melissa glanced in their direction and saw Benjamín approaching the group. He smiled and waved in her direction.

"Come on, Wendy. You know what they say, `if you can't beat 'em, join 'em´."

Wendy sighed, she had no desire to join the group but she was thirsty so she sauntered along with Melissa. She could get a free beer. She still had a full bottle of whiskey hidden in the caravan. That would do for later.

Later that evening, the tiny caravan was alive with activity as three of the four girls fought for the bathroom and tried to prepare for their dates. Wendy tucked herself into the corner of her bed, keeping out of the way. Melissa hogged the only mirror in the bathroom, pausing every couple of minutes to wipe away the condensation that insisted on misting up the mirror from the three hot showers it had just endured. Sara sat on her bed juggling her make-up in her lap and squinting into a tiny hand mirror, while Lisa jumped from one foot to the other as though she were pressing grapes, silently willing one of them to finish.

Melissa emerged from the bathroom and immediately there was a knock on the door. She reached forwards, opening it, expecting Benjamín but found Fernando smiling up at her.

"Hello, Fernando, nice to see you," she said. "Sarah, it's for you."

Sarah grappled with the rest of her make-up and rammed it all into her bag. "I'm ready," she said and headed for the door.

Minutes later, Mario and Benjamín arrived together. They joked and laughed with each other outside while the girls danced around one another, trying to grab their bags. As they finally left surrounded by laughter, sexual tension and the excitement of the unknown, Wendy let out a long, contented sigh.

"Finally! We are alone at last, Jack," she said. Stepping towards the tiny wardrobe, she lifted out the loose base and took out her secret stash of Jack Daniels.

~

Sarah walked in silence across the field with Fernando. He walked with long strides across the field, his hands pushed firmly in his pockets.

"So where do you want to go?"

"No idea!" she replied, feeling slightly unnerved. She had wrongly assumed that he would have planned the evening down to the last detail. Then, she remembered that they had only just arrived in the town. How would he possibly know where to go?

He glanced towards her. "Do you want to eat?"

"That would be nice."

They set off walking; following the traffic signs and heading towards the most brightly lit area they could see. Fifteen minutes later they approached the town centre.

"This place looks nice," Fernando surprised Sarah by taking hold of her hand. "Shall we eat here?"

Sarah looked at the small café restaurant and nodded. "Yeah," she replied. Looking down at his hand in hers, she wondered why she did not feel even the slightest inkling of desire.

∽

Melissa was surprised to find a taxi waiting for them at the entrance.

"So are you hungry?" Benjamín asked as he helped her inside.

"Starving," Melissa replied.

"Well, I must admit that I don't know the town very well, so we'll have to see what we can find."

"Fine."

Inside the cab, Benjamín took her hand and gently squeezed it. "Are you warm enough?"

"Yes." She thought it was a strange question as the taxi did not seem to have an air-con and the warm, Brazilian evening was anything but cold. Her mind was working overdrive. Should she have said no? Had he asked her so that he could put his arm around her? She was unsure and could have kicked herself for her own stupidity.

"So, you have been here a while now, what's your opinion of the circus?"

"I love it!" Melissa replied. "I like the feeling of family," she said, deciding not to mention that she felt that the rest of the women on the show despised her and that she had hated every single minute of the build-up and pull down.

Benjamín smiled. "They are good people. They work hard." He told the taxi driver to pull over.

Melissa returned the smile and exited the taxi. She wanted to say that not everyone worked hard and that it did not seem fair that Sienna did nothing to help, but she decided to keep quiet.

"Do you like Italian food?" He pointed to a tiny bistro bedecked with Italian flags outside. Through the window, Melissa could see the tables covered in red and white checked tablecloths, a vase of real flowers on every table, and the faint tinkle of traditional music drifted towards them.

"That sounds like a great idea," she said.

∼

Lisa walked along the High Street with Mario, looking in the shop windows and admiring different merchandise on display until they came across a fast food joint.

"Hey, do you fancy a burger?" Mario grinned.

"Sure."

He took her hand while they stood waiting their turn in the queue. Lisa smiled.

"I'll get two burgers and we can share some fries," he grinned and winked at her.

Lisa basked in her own happiness, convinced that Mario liked her as much as she liked him.

∼

The following morning, Sarah and Melissa woke up at the same time. They looked at each other from either end of the caravan and smiled.

"How was your date?" Melissa whispered, not wanting to wake Wendy.

"A bit weird, to be honest."

"In what way?"

Sarah let out a deep sigh. "Well, there's just nothing there."

Melissa giggled. "I beg your pardon?"

Sarah laughed. "Sorry, no, I mean that I just don't really have any feelings for him. Don't get me wrong, he's a nice guy, but I'm just not into him, romantically. I guess I have been following our code to the letter. He lives alone, he's got a nice trailer and, I know it sounds bad, but I feel like I'm just using him."

"That's a shame."

"I know," Sarah shrugged. "But I really want to get out of this rust bucket, and I also want to further my career, so if that means hanging out with Fernando and learning the trapeze then I'll do whatever's necessary. Do you think that's wrong of me?"

Melissa paused, slightly lost for words. She could not imagine stringing someone along for her own gain. She knew she was a hopeless romantic, and, for her, Benjamín ticked all the right boxes. She had had a great evening last night, but she still wanted to play it cool. She had no intention of getting embroiled with another married man. She would never purposely put herself in Sarah's position, but she needed to be diplomatic for her friend's sake. "No, I don't think it's wrong. I guess you have to do what's right for you."

Sarah nodded. "What about you? How did it go?"

"It was lovely, actually. We ate in a little Italian Bistro and then we went to a bar for a couple of drinks. He invited me back to his trailer, but I said no."

"Why?"

"I just don't want to move too fast. To be honest, I just want to take things slowly."

Sarah pointed to the empty spot next to Melissa. "It doesn't look like Lisa is in the same frame of mind."

Melissa laughed. "Obviously not!"

"I've got the munchies," Sara replied. "Shall we leave Wendy to sleep and go out for some breakfast? I saw a little bakery on the corner as we were leaving last night."

"Sounds great!"

As the door closed, signally their exit, Wendy stirred. She ran a furry tongue over her teeth. Her mouth felt like a small rodent had climbed inside and died. Her head felt like she had slept with a pile of bricks on her forehead and she desperately wanted to pee. A groan escaped from her lips as she dragged herself out of bed and headed for the toilet. She brushed her teeth with vigour to expel all trace of alcohol and then she put some water in a pan, sat on the bed, and waited for the water to boil. Heaping a spoonful of coffee into a mug, she hesitated only a second before extracting the remains of the Jack Daniels bottle from inside the wardrobe. "Hair of the dog!" she said to herself and poured a decent measure into the cup.

She heard someone fumbling with the front door and swiftly put the bottle under the bed. The quickness of her movement caused her head to spin, and she fell awkwardly onto the bed. As Lisa poked her head inside and looked around the caravan with apprehension, Wendy appeared to be just sitting up.

"Morning..." Lisa said sheepishly. "Where are the others?" She hoped her voice did not sound too cheerful, but she was hoping that she was not the only person to have stayed out all night.

"No idea," Wendy lied. "I'm just making coffee; do you want one?"

"Ooh, yes please, that would be great."

"Good night was it?" Wendy prepared a second cup, poured the boiling water and added milk, all without making eye contact. She did not want to frighten the little mouse, but she would like to know all the gory details.

Lisa smiled. "Yes. I had a great time."

"So, when will you be moving out?" Wendy's acerbic humour was lost on Lisa.

"Well, obviously I stayed there last night, but I didn't have sex if that's what you're thinking! I just slept there, as in, I went to sleep, you know, nothing else." He's got his own caravan behind his parents'. I stayed there.

"Yeah, yeah, Lisa, I get where you're coming from," Wendy said aloud – *and I wish you'd bloody go back there,* she thought.

"I mean, I'm not planning to live there any time soon, you know? At least not yet, anyway."

"Oh, that's a bummer!" Wendy took a large swig of her alcohol-laced beverage and winced. "Because I really need you out of here."

Lisa was instantly offended, "Why me in particular?"

"Oh, don't get me wrong, it's nothing personal. I want you all out; but seeing as you were the first to stay out all night, I assume you'll be the first to leave."

Lisa frowned. She was incapable of reading Wendy's tone and body language, but she felt decidedly uncomfortable. "I'm going for a shower," she said and retreated into the bathroom.

Wendy topped up the coffee mug with more whiskey and settled back on the bed.

"*What the hell am I doing here?*" she asked herself dejectedly.

CHAPTER SIX

The following Sunday after the show, the circus was on the move again. Alfonso, the driver came to collect the girls. Once again, he found them dithering in and out of the caravan and nowhere near ready for him to hitch up their wagon onto the back of his car. He stood with his hands on his hips, shaking his head at their incompetence.

Knowing they were being observed made them even more nervous. Lisa had managed to raise the two back legs. She threw the cranking iron on the grass and ran around to the front to secure the jockey wheel. Wendy picked up the cranking iron with one hand and stood tapping it in the palm of her other hand. Deep in thought, she was oblivious to the fact that Lisa was already wandering around the van, searching the ground, looking for the tool. Sara was still inside tying the cupboard doors together, and Melissa was rolling cables and water pipes.

Alfonso put his hands on his hip, lowered his head and shook it in exasperation.

"All these jobs need to be done during the day," he admonished. "Not now! You should be ready to go now."

The girls avoided eye contact with their disgruntled driver and continued their task as quickly as they could. Alfonso shook his head again as the girls ran around like clowns in a slapstick comedy routine, apologising for the delay.

"I don't believe it, I just don't believe it," Alfonso muttered. "Forget it! I will take the Chinese," he said and stomped off to the next caravan.

The Asians who had been sitting outside their caravan watching the scene with boredom stood up and helped Alfonso to hitch their trailer to the back of his car.

"Sods!" Sarah barked as she watched them. "They could have bloody well helped us!" She threw down her gloves and marched over to the car. "What time will you be back for us?" she said, peering into the driver's side window.

Alfonso glanced at his watch with a casualness that galled Sarah even more.

"Two o'clock, maybe four," he replied. Releasing the handbrake, he told her to move back.

Sarah stomped back to the caravan, threw her gloves inside, sat on the step, and emitted a theatrical sigh.

"What did he say?" Lisa asked.

"Huh! He said two o'clock in the morning or maybe four!"

"Right then!" Wendy clapped her hands together. "There's only one thing for it."

"What?" Melissa asked.

"It's time to party!" Wendy went back inside the van, clambered over the water pipe and cable, straddled the gas bottle, manoeuvred around the stacked up folding chairs, and the other stuff placed on the floor for 'safely'. When she came back out, she was carrying two, five-litre bottles of wine.

"Where did you get those?" Lisa asked, grinning as if she'd just found out she would never have to do another pulldown as long as she lived.

Wendy evaded the question. "Get the chairs out, Lisa. Sarah, there's some crisps and peanuts in the cupboards..."

"The cupboards I've just tied together, I suppose you mean?"

Wendy ignored the sarcastic comment. "And Melissa, you get the glasses."

Lisa began passing the chairs out from the caravan door. "Here," she said, passing one to Wendy.

Wendy placed the wine bottles on the ground with some reverence and opened the chair. "Let the party begin!"

∽

True to his word, Alfonso arrived at four o'clock in the morning and was not amused to find the foursome half asleep in fold-up chairs. By this time, the girls were anything but sober. The nibbles had all gone, and they were starving. Due to their exhaustion, they could not be bothered to drag the gas bottle back outside, hook it up to the connector and cook something substantial. The limited floor space, littered with various other objects, made cooking or doing anything in there seem like an unpassable obstacle course.

Alfonso stood shaking his head yet again as he waited for the girls to get their stuff together. He was in no mood to oblige when they asked him for several comfort stops on the way to the new site. It seemed that, throughout the journey, at least one of them needed the toilet to expel the excess alcohol from one orifice or another!

By the time they all arrived at the next site, the alcohol was beginning to wear off and tempers were frayed due to the lack of sleep, coupled with the knowledge that, within two hours, Martina would be banging on their door to help with the build-up.

Melissa clambered out of the car and stared out into the dawn's morning light to admire the view from their new location. Their van was pushed into position by some of the ring boys, and their new home was destined to be on the outer circle of the travelling caravans.

Their trailer almost touched a long line of forest trees thick with foliage, and at their base, huge bushes and weeds stretched upwards from the shadows, towards the sky, searching for the light.

Lisa watched Melissa's expression turn from tired and fed up to serene and calm. "Nice huh?"

"Yeah, it's really beautiful."

Wendy viewed the scene through more dubious eyes and shivered. "It all looks a bit sinister to me. I wouldn't like to think that there's anything out there in the dead of night."

Sarah laughed. "What? Like zombies and vampires?"

Wendy's eyes narrowed as the others giggled. "No. Actually, I was thinking more about serial killers and lunatics."

The laughing ceased with an abruptness that highlighted the fact that they would be enclosed within a thin, metal box with a decidedly dodgy lock, on a weak and wonky door. Wendy's eyes narrowed with malicious contentment. "Let's hope it doesn't come to that!"

The others watched her enter the caravan, heard her climb over the cables, hosepipe and gas bottle before throwing herself on the bed. "Come on hurry up!" Wendy shouted from the confines of the van. "We've got about two hours of shut-eye before sergeant major Martina comes to bellow at us." They heard the distinctive clump of her shoes as they hit the floor; the creak of old wood panels as she climbed into bed and the throes of a deep sigh as she pulled the covers right over her head.

Melissa looked at the others. "She's got a point. I think we should try to sleep."

Within five minutes the girls were under the covers, fully clothed and half asleep. No-one heard the distinct snapping of twigs underfoot. They were unaware that their van was being monitored from behind a tall, lustrous bush in the undergrowth.

∼

After build-up had been completed, Sienna appeared as if by magic. Apart from the obligatory clogs that all circus performers wore during the day, she could have been mistaken for a Kardashian. In full make-up, designer clothes, and Gucci sunglasses she looked totally out of place as she waved both arms, gathering her dishevelled entourage together. In stark contrast, they stood in dusty, broken footwear, smears of grime adorned every face, their oldest clothes hung limp and torn on their tired bodies and they held up gloved hands to shield their eyes from the sun.

Sienna removed her sunglasses with one flick of a wrist and sucked one earpiece as though she were drawing on a thin lollipop. "At four o'clock I want all of you girls together in the ring. We are going to learn new routines for the show in Rio, and Edwaldo will also choose the girls for his magic act." She glanced at her watch. "That will give you plenty of time to shower, eat, and rest before we start."

When there was no response from the women in front of her, Sienna repositioned her sunglasses and ran a disenchanted eye over her not so loyal subjects. "Beh...ciao!" She turned, her long, blonde hair flicking out and twirling after her like a model in a shampoo advert, and then she picked her way through the site, deftly missing the patches of bald grass and muddy puddles her subjects had been wading through all morning.

Wendy snarled, a deep guttural growl only loud enough for her friends to hear. "The more I see her, the more I want to wipe that bloody, stupid smile off her smug, Italian face!"

Lisa giggled. The other two grinned.

"I know exactly what you mean," Sarah replied. "She's so full of herself, I'd love to rugby tackle her and see her sprawling in the mud!"

"Ooh! Sexy!" Wendy replied suggestively.

Sarah looked away.

"Come on," Melissa grinned. "Let's get a move on, or we'll never be ready for four o'clock."

That afternoon, everyone stood waiting impatiently in the ring for Sienna to put in an appearance. The mismatched group of artists' wives, girlfriends, and significant others stood huddled together at one side of the ring, glancing intermittently across to the four, English girls at the other side of the enclosure.

Wendy smirked, "I've just realised, who they are!"

"What do you mean?" Lisa asked.

"They are the South American equivalent of the English WAGs."

Sarah and Melissa laughed; Lisa looked confused.

"They're what? What does that even mean?" she snapped.

"Jesus, Lisa, where have you been living? WAGs is an acronym..." Wendy replied.

"A what?"

Wendy rolled her eyes towards the top of the tent and shook her head. "Bloody hell, Lisa! An acronym is an abbreviation of several words that are shortened to their first letters and sometimes produce another word."

Lisa's vexed expression, coupled with her profound silence was enough to convince the girls she was even more confused than ever.

"Okay, let's see... for example, NASA, that's short for National Aeronautics and Space Administration. Or BAFTA, that means the British Academy of Film and Television Arts, or CID the Criminal Investigation Department, or AIDS that stands for...well, you get the gist."

"Oh, I get it, so what does WAGs stand for?"

"'Wives and Girlfriends'."

"Bloody hell!" Melissa's expletive caused the other three girls to look in her direction. "Look at the way they're looking us up and down. I feel like we're reliving our first ever encounter with them all over again."

"God help us!" Sarah replied.

"I feel like we are in the cast of 'Westside Story'! Two opposing gangs, fighting out of ignorance rather than understanding," Wendy said. She fanned out her hands at either side of her face and inclined her head for added theatrical effect.

Lisa grinned. "Which gang are we? The sharks or the Jets? Can we be the Sharks?" she asked when nobody replied.

"Look at their faces," Sarah whispered. "They don't exactly look please to be here."

"Well, let's be honest, they already know that we're going to do the big illusions and they'll get all the menial jobs to do. To be honest, I'd be pissed off too," Melissa replied.

"Yeah, I mean, you can't blame them," Wendy sniffed. "After all, this is our only day off. Everyone wants to chill out, relax, and prepare themselves for the rest of the week, yet here we all are buggering about waiting for 'Princess Sienna' to put in an appearance."

The others laughed, which only managed to augment the animosity emanating from the other group.

Lisa sighed. "Great! Now they think we're laughing at them!"

Wendy began circling her friends, with each step she took, she bent her knees and clicked her fingers. "When you're a Jet..."

Melissa grabbed her arm, pulled her closer, and motioned her to stop. Wendy followed her eyes and realised that Sienna had entered the tent. A tall, slim man walked at her side. His long, black coat was sleek and well-cut. Like Sienna, the only aspect of his visage which seemed out of place was the cumbersome, luminous, green clogs on his feet. He had short, black, sleeked back hair, olive skin, high cheekbones and a dazzling, white smile which had appeared as he watched Wendy practising her moves.

Sienna scowled in Wendy's direction, she was far from being amused. She shook her head and held out a hand so that her male counterpart could help her into the ring.

"Oh, for Fuck's sake!" Wendy muttered. "She's been working in circus her whole bloody life; do you really mean to tell me that she can't climb over the ring-fences?" She looked from girl to girl, but they refrained from comment and cast their eyes towards the sawdust at their feet.

"Pathetic!" her interjection came out rather louder than she intended and echoed around the tent like a trapped bird trying to find its way out.

Sienna slammed the stereo system down with annoyance, assuming correctly that the comment was meant for her.

The girls continued to study the sawdust, unsure if Wendy's insult was meant to incorporate them too.

The huddled group at the other side of the ring shuffled closer together with short, indecisive steps and mumbled expletives of their own.

Sienna clapped her hands and addressed them all. "This is Lorenzo; he is a famous choreographer in my home country of Italy. He has graciously decided to come and choreograph the routines for the Theatre Show in Rio de Janeiro."

Lorenzo removed his long coat to reveal his not so splendorous form swathed from head to toe in black lycra. He was as thin as a tomato cane. At his waist was a braided belt made from red and white strips of lycra plaited together that hung in two tassels at the ends - a throwback to the early eighties. He swapped his green clogs for a pair of black jazz shoes; stood erect and clapped his hands together once. "Buon pomeriggio," he grinned, perusing each stunned face in front of him.

"Here we go then," Melissa muttered. "Let's hope his choreography is more up to date than his workout gear!"

"I have a sneaking suspicion that it won't be," Sarah replied.

"Okay girls, follow me," Lorenzo ordered. He split all the members in the ring into two groups and positioned them at either side of the stage. "So, you will enter the ring in two lines. One from the left and one from the right. Follow me, follow me. And... step ball change, step ball change, step click, step click, turn... and turn, and turn, and flick ball change."

Wendy looked at Sarah and sighed with disillusion. "Yeah, it looks like you're right. His idea of choreography went out with the ark!"

The others smothered their giggles and mirrored his choreography with ease. The WAGs, on the other hand, fumbled their way through the routine, complained at the difficulty and asked each other for help.

Over the next three hours, Lorenzo fashioned the divergent group into some semblance of a nineteen-eighties dance troupe. The animosity between the Sharks and the Jets augmented as the English Sharks were given prime positions, once again, at the front of the new routines and the Jets were relegated to be background fodder.

This time, Wendy kept her mouth firmly closed. The Jets were doing enough cursing and muttering for everyone.

Lorenzo had just allocated standing positions around the ring for the Jets and called the Sharks to the front when the ring doors opened and Edwaldo came marching into the ring.

Sienna flashed him a dazzling smile and put her hand to her mouth to throw him an exaggerated, theatrical kiss as he approached.

He nodded in recognition but did not reciprocate the gesture. He looked slightly annoyed by the open show of affection.

An entourage of ring-boys scurried behind him or emerged from backstage carrying and pushing an amalgam of magic props of various shapes and sizes. Edwaldo barked orders while they attempted to position various pieces around the ring. The entire dance group was forced into the centre where they stood like trapped cattle in a holding pen.

Edwaldo stood at the front with Sienna and Lorenzo, one hand rested on his chin as he perused the motley crew before him. He muttered ideas and suggestions to Sienna, pointing weakly at certain females or flicking a lazy hand in their direction. Sienna seemed to have the final say. She nodded or shook her head to each idea, revelling in her sense of power.

"Is it my imagination, or is Sienna shaking her head whenever he points in my direction?" Wendy said under her breath.

"Uh-huh," Lisa said, sotto voce.

"Er, that would be a yes," Melissa replied as Sarah gave a slight nod.

"Huh! That's just great!" Wendy folded her arms across her chest and tried to appear nonplussed.

As the selection process continued, everyone was made aware that Sienna would also be taking part in the magic spectacular. She was going to be performing all the smaller tricks and leaving the larger illusions to her husband. Each time they started on a new trick, they perused the line of dancers with critical precision. Whispering and muttering to themselves accompanied by lots of head shaking or nodding. Their actions made each chosen female feel relieved to have been elected and removed from the cattle pen.

"I hate this!" Sarah complained. "I feel like I'm back at school, and they're picking teams for a hockey match. I don't want to still be here when we get down to the final two!"

The hours ticked by and, regardless of whether they had been chosen or not, everyone was forced to stay and watch the proceedings. Almost all the entire male members of the circus had invaded the tent, to see what was keeping their other halves from preparing dinner. The men watched with angry expressions as Edwaldo ran his hands around their partners' waists or shoulders to position them correctly on stage or in an illusion. As time rolled by, the artists and dancers sat around the ring, tired, bored, and hungry. The Sharks (apart from Wendy) were allocated the prime illusions. Melissa and Sarah were put through their paces. They were taught by Edwaldo under the gruelling, watch of Sienna. Lisa was told what trick she would be performing, but she wasn't given any practice time, which made her truculent and childlike.

"Why does she always have to perform the illusions first?" Lisa grumbled. "It's just wasting more time!"

"Because she wants everyone to know that she knows how everything is done. She's done it before, and she wants you to know that you are not the first, and probably won't be the last, to step into her shoes in the ring," Wendy explained.

Sarah nodded. "I also think that although she is showing us how to do the trick, and what it's supposed to look like, she's here to keep an eye on her husband."

"How do you mean?" Lisa asked.

"I don't think she has any intention of letting some waif of a dancer usurp her from her role as the most important female on the entire show."

An hour later, at almost midnight, Edwaldo clapped his hands together to get everyone's attention. "Okay, so everyone knows what they will be doing and what magic they are involved in. I will send messages throughout this week so that you can come to the ring to practise. As for now, we'll finish."

There was a lot of shuffling, mumbling and sighing as everyone exited from the side doors or backstage exit and headed back to their allocated vans.

While the other three raved about Zig-zag illusions, sub trunk illusions, and Water Cascade illusions, Wendy was seething. Due to pissing off Sienna earlier in the afternoon, Wendy had the great task of walking on stage and holding a small wooden tray. Sienna threw a pair of white gloves onto it and the gloves were transformed into a white dove. Wendy would be on stage for the great amount of about twenty seconds.

"Shall I make some pasta?" Melissa suggested, holding up a pan and a wooden spoon as though she were about to perform another magic trick.

"I'm too tired to eat," Sarah sank onto her bed and sighed.

"I'll just have a bag of crisps," Lisa waved a large bag of Brazilian brand chips.

Wendy unscrewed a new bottle of Jack Daniels and ferreted around the tiny cupboard in search of a glass. "I'm going to console myself with Jack."

As the others fell asleep, Wendy sat on her fold-up chair outside the caravan. She listened to the mumbled conversations coming from the surrounding trailers, the gentle light filtering through the thin curtains gave the night a fairylike ambiance. The smell of various meals cooking over tiny stoves made her mouth water, but she could not be bothered to fix herself anything to eat, and she did not want to disturb the others. Contemplating the meaning of life and how hers had drastically veered off from her chosen path, she jumped when a loud crack from the forest behind her made her sit up straight and pay attention. Her instincts told her to flee, the hair on her neck stood to attention and she felt as though she were being watched. She stood up and peered around the side of the van into the forest. *What wild animals are there in Brazil?* She thought. She had no idea. The snap of another branch forced her to take action. Grabbing the bottle and abandoning her chair, she jumped inside the van, locking the door behind her.

~

The following morning, the girls were awoken by a harsh knocking on the door.

"Go away!" Wendy shouted, then she cradled her head with her two arms to lessen the pain that rang through her temple and brain.

"What's going on?" Lisa pulled herself to a sitting position, rubbed tired eyes, and tried to focus on the door.

Melissa crawled over her, opened the door and squinted in the bright sunlight. "Yes?" she said, staring at one of the Ring-boys whose agitation was more than evident. He flicked his eyes from left to right, uncomfortable to be seen loitering by the girls' caravan.

"Lisa has rehearsal now. Hurry, hurry!" He sprinted away as though it was a matter of great urgency.

Melissa turned to Lisa, "Did you hear that? Rehearsal, now!"

Lisa flopped back onto the pillow. "Great! That's just what I wanted to hear...NOT!"

While she freshened herself up in the tiny bathroom and pulled on some clothes, Melissa prepared a hasty cup of coffee and pushed three biscuits into her hand.

"Here, eat these, to keep your strength up."

"Thanks," Lisa took the offerings with a grateful smile.

When she arrived in the tent, the huge water illusion stood centre stage. Edwaldo stood explaining something to four Ring-boys who stood like soldiers at ease with their hands clasped firmly behind their backs, nodding in recognition to the boss.

"Ah. Lisa," he said, extenuating the first vowel sound so her name sounded like 'Lee-za'. He held out a hand in greeting and smiled. "Come, come."

Lisa returned the smile, wondering whether to correct him on the pronunciation of her name. She decided against it. She walked into the ring, intrigued to learn what she was supposed to do in the illusion and ruminating on the possible whereabouts of Sienna. Lisa had assumed that the Circus Princess would be giving her a demonstration as she had done with everyone else the day before. Her mind wandered back to the previous day when she had been chosen for the illusion. Edwaldo had merely flipped a hand over in the direction of the magic trick and said: "You will do that." She wondered if Sienna had ever performed the illusion. Maybe that was why she had not put in an appearance because she had no idea how it worked.

When it became apparent that Sienna would not be gracing them all with her presence, Lisa tried to listen intently to everything that Edwaldo said. She wanted to understand exactly what it was she was expected to do.

"First you put this on," Edwaldo held out something which looked like a metal harness and reminded Lisa of a baby swing at the park. As Edwaldo held it and bend towards her, Lisa placed her hands on both his shoulders and stepped into it. At that moment, the doors to the tent burst open, and in strode Mario. He came to a stop, eyed the scene with his hands on both hips and glared at Lisa, anger dripping from every pore like a leaking tap.

Edwaldo, oblivious to the silent yet electric scene playing out before him, ran his hands around her waist to fasted the belt in place. He stood back to view his handy-work and at that point, he realised that there was a silent stand-off between his new assistant and the young trapeze artist. He guessed there must be some chemistry going on between the two. He had seen the envious looks of possessive jealousy many times over the years, from his hot-blooded, male performers. "Ah, Mario, what do you think?" he said, in an attempt to break the tension. "Lisa will be the star of the show in Rio. She is going to do the water illusion with me."

He saw Lisa flash a weary smile in Mario's direction, which was not returned.

"Genial," Mario's choice of word was not matched by his unenthusiastic tone. He forced a smile through his lips in the boss' direction, shoved his hands into his pockets and sauntered out of the tent.

"What does 'Hen-ee-al' mean, Lisa's shy little voice made Edwaldo smile.

"It means, 'great'." He saw her crestfallen expression and lifted her chin with a gentle hand. "Don't worry, little one," he smiled. "Everything will be fine."

Sienna who had entered from the side door did not smile. She had seen that expression on her husband's face before. She would have to keep an eye on him and that stupid girl or he would be taking another lover and Sienna was not prepared to stand for it again.

∼

After the practise, Lisa ran off to try and find Mario. She tried his caravan, but he was not home. When she approached his parents' trailer her run trailed to slow, leaden footsteps. She paused and then knocked with a tentative fist on the door. She saw the caravan lurch from left to right as the bulk of Mario's mum, Maria, swung herself to a standing position and waddled towards the door.

"Er...Mario?" Lisa inquired as the door inched open.

His mother studied her through narrowed eyes before turning to look back inside the caravan. Her eyes focused on someone or something before she turned back to Lisa.

"No está."

Lisa felt sure that she was lying and that Mario was hiding from her inside the trailer. He just did not want to speak to her.

"Oh, okay," she forced a weak smile in the monster's direction and skittered away like a frightened deer. Her mind was in turmoil. Surely he must see that if she was practising in the ring, where anyone could walk in, she was hardly likely to be flirting with the owner of the show. In fact, she would not dare to flirt with him. She would not want to face the wrath of Princess Sienna. She also did not find him in the least bit attractive.

She arrived at her caravan and opened the door.

"What's up with you? Why the long face?" Wendy asked, "Is the illusion difficult or something?"

"No, it's Mario. He came into the ring, and he didn't like the fact that Edwaldo was helping me put the harness on."

"Ah, that's nothing," Wendy flicked a wrist and shook her head dismissively. "He'll get over it. He's bound to be a bit jealous. He thought you were all his, and now he finds you being `dressed´, as it were, by the owner of the circus no less. He'll get over it." She repeated. "Don't worry about it."

Melissa placed a hand on Lisa's shoulder. "Wendy's right. You can explain to him what's happening and he'll be fine."

"Ooh, young love," Sarah crooned, trying to make Lisa laugh, but failing. "They're right though, Lisa. Try not to worry. Everything will be fine."

"That reminds me," Lisa said, pointing in Sarah's direction, "Edwaldo is waiting for you in the ring."

"Oh, shit!" Sarah replied.

The others giggled at her discomfort.

∼

After the show, Lisa was still worrying about Mario and his lack of attention to her. She had glanced several times in his direction during the performance, but he had avoided all eye contact. At one point, she had even attempted to walk over to him, but he had seen her coming and had headed off in the opposite direction. She sat down on the bed, deep in thought, wringing her hands together.

The girls recognised her behaviour as her way of releasing stress. Melissa looked at her with concern. "Don't worry about him so much, Lisa, he'll come around, they always do."

Sarah nodded. "Listen to Melissa, Lisa. It's true."

Wendy looked at the three of them and snorted. "These Latin American men are all the same. It only takes one wrong look or one wrong move and BANG! You in their bad books."

Lisa looked in Wendy's direction for conformation.

"Believe me," Wendy waved a ham and cheese sandwich toward her to emphasise her point. "After all, I should know, I'm still married to one!"

"WHAT!" The girls cried in unison.

"You're married?" Sarah's mouth hung open in shock.

"Close your mouth, you look like you're catching flies," Wendy chomped down on her sandwich and viewed their surprised expressions with fascination.

"I had no idea," Melissa muttered, continuing to stare with rapt surprise.

"Yeah, well, there's a lot you don't know about me."

"So, what are you doing here?" Lisa sat down on her bed and stared at Wendy as though it was the first time she had set eyes on such an unusual creature. Her own predicament was temporarily forgotten.

Wendy thought back to Lisa's idealised conceptions of circus life.

"I did what everyone did in all the books you've read, Lisa, I ran away with the circus."

Sarah sat down next to Lisa.

Melissa soon followed. "But why?"

"Because my husband is a real evil bastard, that's why." Wendy looked at her three roommates and felt like she was giving a lecture on the evils of marriage. "To cut a long story short, he was mixed up in the drug trade, but I didn't know that when I married him. We had money, a lot of it in fact, but I had no idea where it came from. I thought he had a normal job. He left the house every morning in a suit and tie. I mean, how was I supposed to know that it was just a front!" Her final utterance was a statement rather than a question.

"So what happened?" Lisa could not help but think that marrying a man with money could not be all bad.

"Well, he committed a drug dealer's cardinal sin. He began dabbling with his merchandise, didn't he? The more he took, the more violent and possessive he became. The first time he hit me, I forgave him. You see, I was still oblivious to what was going on, and I assumed he was under pressure at work. But, as time went on, I became a prisoner in my own house. I wasn't allowed out – not that I would have gone anyway because I was covered in bruises from head to toe. When I found out that he was cutting the drugs with poor-quality substitutes I knew I had to get out. I knew I could be in danger. If the Big Boss found out, he could take his revenge out, not only on my husband but on me too."

"So, what did you do?" Lisa sat perched on the edge of the bed, totally engrossed in the incredible story, not quite believing what she was hearing.

"I started squirrelling money away. He had so much, he didn't miss it. I could take a hundred dollars out of his wallet when he was in the shower and he'd never even realise it. I had no idea where I was going to go or what I was going to do, I just knew that I had to get away. Then one day, while he was out, I was on the internet and I got in contact with an old dancing colleague of mine. She told me about this job and my mind was made up. What better way to lose someone than by travelling around? And in a totally different country."

"But, how did you get to the audition?" Melissa asked.

"I didn't do the audition. I decided to confide in my friend Rachael and she said she'd do everything she could to help. Rachael knew the choreographer and she persuaded her to give me the job on her recommendation."

"Wow! So then what happened?" Sarah asked.

"Then I began to store clothes so that when the time was right I could just leave."

"Is that why you were so nervous on the plane?" Melissa asked.

"Yeah, with my husband's contacts, I felt like I was sitting on a knife's edge. One small movement and I'd have been cut to ribbons. I was a nervous wreck while the plane sat on the runway. I kept thinking that at any moment, the plane doors would burst open and I'd be ordered off the aircraft."

"Bloody Hell!" Lisa muttered.

"Now you know why I don't want to get involved with anyone here. I've had enough of men. I need time for me, to find myself again and to heal."

Melissa walked the few steps across the caravan to hug Wendy. "I had no idea!"

The other two came to do the same. "Group hug," Sarah said, and they embraced each other in silence.

A minute later Wendy shrugged them off. "Okay, okay, that's enough maudlin, let's have a drink." She reached under her bed and extracted the bottle of whiskey. "Get the ice."

Sarah jumped up and opened the tiny fridge. Melissa silently registered that this was most likely the reason why Wendy drank so much. As Wendy prepared the glasses, Lisa pulled on her jacket and stood awkwardly at the door.

"I'm going to go for a bit of a walk," she said. "I need to clear my head."

Wendy shook her head as they watched Lisa walk off in the direction of Mario's caravan. "You see; you can't teach them anything. Everyone has to make their own mistakes. I wouldn't listen to my mother. She told me to stay away, but I was..." she lifted her hands to the sides of her head to imitate inverted commas, "in love." She shook her head, "what an idiot!"

Melissa and Sarah were unsure whether Wendy was referring to herself or Lisa, but the comment seemed appropriate for both of them.

∼

Lisa held her jacket closed with both hands, the temperature had dropped drastically compared with the day's sunshine. A swirly, grey mist had fallen around the circus, enshrouding it with an ethereal ambience that sent shivers down her spine and made the thought of confronting Mario much more daunting. His van stood in darkness, so she headed over to his parent's trailer and tapped lightly on the door. She waited for the lurch and groan of the caravan. Mario's mother opened the door and eyed her with open contempt that made Lisa feel as though the woman could shrink people at a mere glance.

"Er...Mario?"

His mother let her stew in her own discomfort for a few seconds before she shook her head. "No. Party." She raised an obese arm and pointed to the far end of the field with a podgy finger.

Across the road, a huge establishment stood out against the night sky. The eerie sound of the bass guitar droned into the night, and the steady beat of drums gave the impression that the establishment was pulsating. Flashing lights and a neon sign of a topless dancer flashed into the murky night like a lighthouse beacon, welcoming men home.

Lisa looked back at Mario's mother and gave her a weak, uncertain smile. "Er... okay, thank-you, er...gracias!" She spun on her heels and walked towards her caravan. Midway there, she stopped. She had no desire to return yet. Wendy's tale had distressed her. She knew that Wendy had told the story for two reasons. Firstly, to get it off her chest and secondly, Wendy wanted to warn her to be careful. Lisa felt slightly disgruntled. Just because Wendy had gone through a bad experience didn't mean to say that all Latin men were the same... or did it? Lisa was sure that Mario would not hit her, but if his behaviour today was anything to go by, he was certainly moody. All she wanted to do was have the chance to speak to him and explain that he had got the wrong idea.

She decided to head over towards the establishment and see if she could see him. Not wanting or daring to go inside, she planned to linger for a while and see if he was outside. She reached the edge of the field and was about to cross the deserted road when male laughter echoed behind her. She stopped, frozen to the spot. Instinctively, she jumped behind the nearest tree. Seconds later, a group of male artists crossed the road laughing and bantering between themselves, patting each other on the back, nudging elbows into ribs and acting like adolescents.

Lisa did not recognise them all, due to the undulating rolls of mist, but she was surprised to see Edwaldo among the group. As they headed towards the swing doors, they opened with a bang as one door slammed into the wall with a resounding crash. Lisa gasped. Mario was exiting with his arms slung over the shoulders of a call girl, who tottered on drunken heels and pulled her exceedingly short top into position to cover her protruding breasts. Mario stopped to talk to the group of guys, who made it obvious that they were impressed by his selection. They repeated their earlier nudging and back-patting, only this time to Mario, then they pulled away and walked towards the entrance. The beating drums and bass guitar of the latest song drew then inside like a mermaid's siren calling into the night.

Lisa remained hidden behind the tree and watched with augmenting jealousy as Mario crossed the road and headed towards the tent. She wondered why he was taking the girl inside. All the lighting would be off; the girl would not be able to see anything. The tent was only lit by a generator during the shows. A second, separate 'jenny' ran the electric for the caravans. Lisa crept on tip-toe behind them, intrigued to find out what would happen yet feeling physically sick at the same time. Hiding between the vans and other obstacles, she peered into the gloom, watching with envious obsession as Mario pulled up one of the wallings and beckoned the girl to follow him inside.

Close to tears, Lisa faltered, unsure whether to see this through and satisfy her morbid curiosity or leave. She neared the tent and saw that the walling was still pulled up. Taking that as a sign that she should enter, she crawled inside and hid under the tiered seating. Letting her eyes become accustomed to the darkness, her head snapped to the left as the sound of laughter echoed around the empty tent, taunting her. It was coming from backstage. Creeping forwards, picking her way over metal stabilizers and seating rails, she headed towards the side curtains. Once there, she reached out and opened them a sliver with both hands. There, on the acrobats' crash mat, lay Mario and the girl locked in a frenzied embrace. Lisa put her hand to her mouth. Tears stung the backs of her eyes. She wanted to flee, but she found herself frozen to the spot. She watched with horror as Mario ran his hands up and down the girl's body and then rolled on top of her.

Suddenly finding her feet, she let the curtains drop back into place and stumbled through the tent, eyes pricking with yet unshed tears as she ran back to the sanctuary of her caravan.

Wendy was right, she thought. *All men are bad.* Back at the caravan, she was about to turn the key in the door when she heard twigs snapping in the trees behind the caravan. She froze. "Who's there?" she called out into the darkness.

The deathly silence only seemed to highlight her vulnerability, standing alone in the middle of a foggy field in the early hours of the morning.

The door abruptly swung open and the weak, yellow lighting inside impelled her to enter.

"Er...I think we got the joke wrong?" a slurring, swaying Wendy giggled as she beckoned Lisa inside.

Lisa frowned, she was not in the mood for drunken silliness. "What?"

"The joke. We got it wrong! You knocked on the door and said: 'Whose there?' right? But first, you're supposed to say 'knock, knock', and then I'm supposed to say 'who's there'!"

Melissa and Sarah burst into laughter, but Wendy's terrible joke had rather the reverse effect on Lisa. She burst into tears.

CHAPTER SEVEN

THE NEXT MORNING, the girls were awoken by a harsh knocking on the door. Melissa did the honours, holding her head with the palm of her hand as the whiskey from the night before appeared to have found a hammer and was banging it repeatedly against her forehead. She pulled on her dressing gown and peered out into the bright sunlight.

"Yes?"

"You and Sarah, rehearsal in the ring. Come."

A groan echoed from the other side of the van as Sarah tried to sit up.

Melissa scowled at the messenger and tapped the face of her watch with one finger. "Half an hour, okay?"

The messenger scowled. Melissa wondered if he understood, but she was past the point of caring.

She dragged herself into the tiny bathroom and had a cold shower to try and wake herself up. When she came out, the saucepan was boiling water and four mugs generously filed with instant coffee granules stood waiting to be filled. As Melissa left, Sarah stepped into the bathroom and slammed the door. Wendy and Lisa had only managed to half sit up, on each bed.

"Bloody hell, Lisa, you look like some sort of sick panda with those great big, red patches around both your eyes," Wendy quipped. "That's the dastardly result of drinking too much whiskey and crying yourself to sleep."

Lisa tutted, folded her arms across her chest and looked away. She was annoyed with herself for getting into such a state and annoyed with Wendy because she knew that she was right.

Melissa decided not to comment. In her own little world, she wondered what she was going to have to rehearse and for how long. The only thing she wanted to do was to crawl back into bed. She poured the water and passed around the cups. Then she prepared four bowls of cereal and repeated the action. "I feel no more like rehearsing than going to have a tooth filled at the dentists!" Melissa confided.

"Tell me about it," Sarah took the proffered bowl but placed it on the side. "Sorry, but if I eat that, I'll puke!"

"Fair enough," Melissa replied and gave Lisa a second helping. "Come on. Let's head over to the tent. The sooner we get in there; the sooner it'll be over."

They walked across the site with coffee cups in hand. The wallings were risen to air out the tent, so they scooted underneath rather than walk to the nearest door. Edwaldo was in the centre of the ring with his white tiger inside a small cage, which the girls knew was their magic trick.

"Ah, here you are!" Edwaldo held out his hand towards them as they flashed weak smiles in his direction. "Today we practise your trick, okay?"

The girls nodded half-heartedly. During the first rehearsal, they had merely been told to climb into the cage and squat down onto their haunches, holding onto the bars. Once again, Sienna had felt the need to perform the trick first, going through the motions as to how to climb inside a cage while still retaining their femininity – as if they did not already know!

Sarah looked at Melissa in alarm. "Surely he isn't expecting us to get in there with that!" She inclined her head towards the big cat that was pacing around the cage, impatient feet beating the thin, wooden base of the trick with angry paws and giant-sized claws.

All heads turned when one of the side doors opened with a loud rattle and in walked Princess Sienna accompanied by Lorenzo. She would not belittle herself by stooping under a walling. Giving the girls a scathing glance, she held out her hand and waited for the choreographer to help her into the ring.

"Oh for God's sake!" Sara mumbled. "Why does she think she's so bloody important?"

"Let's just keep our mouths shut and get this over with," Melissa replied, clutching her head in an attempt to stop it spinning.

Once again, Sienna felt obliged to show the girls how the trick should be performed. She ordered them to turn their backs so that the illusion could be prepared. When they were allowed to turn back around, the tiger had disappeared and a red cloth was thrown over half of the cage. Sienna paraded herself around the ring, posing and turning, trying to walk like some sort of supermodel, but not quite pulling it off, before climbing elegantly into the cage. Edwaldo closed it and covered the entire trick with the red material. He spun the cage around three times then whipped off the cloth. Sienna had mysteriously disappeared and in her place was the white tiger.

"Impressive," Melissa replied, clapping her hands to show an element of enthusiasm, then wished she had not bothered because the clapping jarred her brain and made her feel dizzy.

Sarah gave a half-hearted thumbs-up when Sienna climbed out of the cage.

"Now it is your turn," Sienna pointed in their direction, but the girls had other ideas. They stood transfixed when one of the ring boys opened the cage with tentative fingers, clipped a lead onto the giant tiger's collar, and attempted to coax it out of the cage.

The girls took several steps backwards as survival instinct kicked in. The mere size of the cat was enough to send both girls leaping over the ring-fence and running for the doors. Edwaldo's laughter followed them, then he shouted at them and told them to come back. The girls turned around and edged forwards towards the ring with slow, tentative steps while two ring-boys manhandled the tiger into a bigger cage.

Sienna's face openly showed her annoyance at their timidity. "Come back here! Let's begin," she snapped. During the next ten minutes, Lorenzo tried to choreograph a short routine for them to enter the ring while the illusion would be brought into position. The looks of pure, unadulterated disbelief rebounded from the eyes of one girl to the other and back again as he concocted a dance routine that a primary student could have easily performed.

"...and step together step clap. And turn... and present the trick."

As he beamed his whiter than white smile, the girls stood open-mouthed unable to comment at the banality of the routine.

Sienna took over. "Then you get into the cage one by one. Melissa, you go first. You enter like this..." While she gave them yet another demonstration, Sarah gave a huge sigh and muttered, "Oh for fuck's sake! I can't take much more of this."

"Hold it together, just hold it together," Melissa advised, gripping Sarah's wrist in a motion of support.

"I thought Lorenzo was supposed to be a top choreographer?" Sarah complained, "What exactly is he top of? Top of the flops?"

Melissa giggled then held her head in pain. "Don't worry, we can choreograph something else later on. Let's just get this over with."

An hour later, when boredom had evaporated their hangovers and they were left giggling at everything Sienna said or Lorenzo did, they were told that they were finally going to do the trick for real.

The cage was prepared, tinny music crackled through the ageing speakers and the girls fought back their laughter while they performed the imbecilic dance routine before climbing into the cage. Edwaldo spun the trick around three times, giving the girls time to hide in the bottom of the trick. As the cloth was removed, they lay flat, squashed together with their legs crossed, under the flimsy, wooden floor. Sarah grabbed Melissa's hand, and they squeezed each other for moral support. Fear stopped any further giggling as the great tiger paced the cage. The insubstantial, thin piece of wood bent under the tiger's heft so that it was inches away from the girl's faces while it walked in circles, waiting to be released and fed.

After what felt like forever, they were released from the trick. Sienna scrutinized their expressions and was pleased by their dishevelled appearance and wide, frightened eyes.

She dismissed them with a flick of her wrist. "Okay, you can go."

∼

Back at the caravan, Wendy gripped the bedding, trying to hold her tongue. Lisa had been moping around all morning and it was getting on her nerves.

"Will you buck up! Stop thinking about him. You look like you've dropped a pound and found a penny. Or should I say dropped some Reales and found a centavo?" she grinned at her conversion joke.

Lisa looked confused. "What?"

"Bloody hell, you really like him, don't you?" Wendy sat opposite her and stared into her watery eyes. She did not wait for a reply. "Look, if it's meant to be, it will be. Don't worry so much. Everything will sort itself out."

"Do you think so?" Lisa's tear-filled eyes pulled at Wendy's heart.

"Yes, I'm sure of it. I tell you what, get dressed and we'll go into town. That should take your mind off things for a while."

Half an hour later, they hit the town centre. Lisa's mood brightened as they perused the shops and tried on various articles of clothing. Wendy was not as enthralled as her companion. She could not shake the niggling feeling that she was being watched. She wanted to ask Lisa if she felt the same but decided against it. This was the first time she'd seen the kid smiling all day, she did not want to dampen her mood. Wendy resorted to casually making intermittent head turns in various directions, but she could not distinguish a particular person.

Lisa, unaware of Wendy's inquietude was grateful for her company. "Shall we have a coffee now?" she said, juggled three bags, each containing articles of clothing that she had been unable to resist.

"Sure."

They sat in the food hall of the mall sipping latte's and eating chocolate muffins. While Lisa chattered inanely, Wendy nodded, half-listening as she scrutinized the crowd. She still could not shake the feeling of being followed. If her husband had found out where she was hiding, there was no doubt in her mind that he would send someone to bring her back. She scrutinised the shoppers and decided that groups of people could be discarded, she felt that her observer would be working alone. There were no people wearing raincoats, dark glasses, and carrying newspapers like she's seen in so many spoof spy films. She knew that she needed to look for someone nondescript, someone who would blend easily into a crowd.

Lisa finally picked up on Wendy's uneasiness. "Is everything okay?"

"Eh? Oh, yeah, everything's fine. Shall we go?" Wendy did not wait for confirmation she was on her feet before she had finished the sentence.

"Oh, er, yeah." Lisa took a final swig of her coffee, stuffed the remaining piece of muffin in her mouth, then dusted her hands together. "Okay. Let's go!"

∽

Melissa and Sarah were surprised to find that the other two had gone out. They pondered over whether to make lunch for the four of them but decided against it. They were tucking into Spaghetti Bolognaise when a second knock on the door disturbed them.

Sarah placed her knife and fork down with a theatrical sigh.

"What is it today with people knocking on the bloody caravan? Are we to have no peace?" She opened the door to find the same ring-boy who had woken them up that morning.

"You again," she sighed, folding her arms across her chest.

"You come to ring now," he said. Glancing inside he pointed an accusing finger in Melissa's direction, "and you."

Sarah emitted a second exaggerated sigh of abject frustration and bent forward so that she was eye level with the messenger. "Ten minutes, okay? Ten minutes! We are eating lunch!"

Wandering over to the tent they discussed what the reason could be for the presence of their company.

"It's probably Sienna. Maybe she made up an even more idiotic dance routine for us to perform than Lorenzo's," Melissa laughed.

"Thank God we're working abroad and nobody we know is going to see the shitty choreography we're being forced to perform."

"Well, as I said before, maybe we can change it once the rehearsals are over, I mean, Sienna won't be able to watch the entire show, and I refuse to be seen doing primary level dance moves."

"Okay, you're on!" Sarah grinned, "That's a cunning plan," she said tapping her fingertips together and looked at Melissa through narrowed eyes.

They were laughing as they entered the ring but stopped when they saw Edwaldo and Benjamín standing in the centre with two ropes hanging from the cupola.

"Are there you are!" Edwaldo held out a hand towards the girls and swung it around to the ropes as though he were presenting them to the entire collection of empty circus seats. "Come, come."

"What's going on?" Sarah looked from one man to the other.

"Benjamín and I have been talking, and we think it would be a good idea if both of you performed the web when we go to Rio."

"WHAT!" the girls said in unison.

"You can perform while the ring boys are setting up for another act below you," Edwaldo explained. "I know from Benjamín that you,

Melissa have had a few lessons, so you, Sarah, will have a bit of catching up to do." He looked at both of them waiting for an answer, but the girls had been stunned into silence. "...So, I've booked the ring for you both. For the next seven days, you will practise after the show."

Sarah looked across at Melissa and grimaced.

"But for now, I am going to help you, Sarah." He pointed in Melissa's direction. "Melissa you continue with Benjamín."

Melissa smiled at Benjamín, unsure how to react in his presence. She was not sure if the circus owner was aware of their relationship or even if he would approve, so she decided to play it cool.

"Melissa, show Sarah how to climb up the rope, please," Edwaldo ordered.

Benjamín steadied the rope and place his hand on her back as she began to climb, his mere touch made her feel light-headed. She was not sure if it was purely from his touch or the combination of a lack of sleep, too much alcohol, the entire morning's rehearsals or the belly full of Spaghetti Bolognaise. She steeled herself to reach the top of the rope and secured her hand in the loop at the top.

"Good, good," Edwaldo placed a hand above his eyes as he watched her climb. Then he turned to Sarah. "Now, my dear, it's your turn."

Sara grasped the rope as though she wanted to strangle it and with a resigned heave on the cord, she began to climb towards the cupola.

∽

Lisa's happiness from her shopping trip slowly diminished during the show when Mario continued to ignore her. To make matters worse, Miguel sauntered over and struck up a conversation. Lisa could not ignore him, but she was inwardly cringing; she could feel Mario's eyes boring into her back the longer they talked.

At the end of the show, she timed it so that she would leave the tent at the same time as Mario. She called his name, but he pretended not to hear her.

"Mario," she said again, catching hold of his arm.

He looked down as though something abhorrent had touched him, then he looked into Lisa's eyes with a cold steel-like stare. "¿Sí?"

"I'm sorry, Mario, but I wasn't doing anything wrong. In fact, if anyone is in the wrong, it's you."

"What?" he removed her hand from his arm with a rough swipe.

"I saw you..." she waited for some reaction but none was forthcoming. She decided to reiterate. "I saw you last night, leaving the nightclub...with a girl."

He threw his arms up into the air and shook his head for several seconds while he thought of a suitable reply. "But, don't you see? That was your fault. You made me do that!"

Lisa frowned and shook her head in total incomprehension. "What?"

"How do you think I felt seeing you throwing yourself at Edwaldo like a bitch, a prostitute."

"He was helping me with the magic trick!" Lisa's voice rose as her blood began to boil over. Nobody had ever called her anything so detrimental and so untrue in her life. She felt the need to retaliate. "If anyone's a prostitute, it's that bitch you slept with last night!"

Mario looked slightly surprised by her outburst. This time the tables were turned. It was his time to reach out for her arm and her turn to shrug him off. She lifted her chin and walked with her head held high out of the tent.

Back at the caravan, she divulged the content of the entire conversation to the other three. Wendy feigned interest better than the other two. Sarah was preparing to return to the ring to practise the web, whereas Melissa was preparing to go out on a date with Benjamín. Wendy was envisaging a quiet night in – preferably alone with her mate Jack Daniels, but with Lisa's latest revelations she doubted that would be on the cards.

Sarah headed for the door, "Good for you, Lisa!" she gave her a thumbs up and headed out. Seconds later, Benjamín's head appeared around the door, "Hola everyone!" he grinned. "Are you ready, Melissa?" He appraised her outfit, tight jeans, a strappy sequined top, and slip-on high-heeled sandals. "You look beautiful."

Melissa blushed. She loved complements but not in front of her friends. "Thank you," she mumbled as she grabbed her clutch bag, said a quick goodbye to the other two, and stepped outside.

It was a beautiful, warm summer evening, even the hint of a listless breeze wafted balmy air around them. They sauntered out of the site, arm in arm, too engrossed in each other to notice a lone figure hiding in the trees, waiting.

They stopped at a bar-restaurant and ate `Feijoada´ a typical Brazilian dish of rich, hearty stew made with pork and black beans.

Benjamín poured the red wine and passed a glass to Melissa, "Salud."

"Cheers."

"I feel so comfortable with you," Benjamín confided. "This is going to sound a bit mushy, but I think that we are meant to be together, you know?"

Melissa nodded and tried to bury her head in her wine glass as much as she could. She was far from comfortable with the conversation. She had strong feelings for Benjamín, but after Wendy's revelation and the announcement that all Latin men were dangerous, Melissa was not ready to pour out her heart and confess her undying love for a man she hardly knew.

Benjamín studied her, he was surprised by his own admission. He had never met anyone quite like Melissa and he was being honest when he professed his feelings, which surprised even him. But now, after pouring out his heart, he looked at Melissa through confused eyes. He thought that she felt the same, but now he was not so sure. He had wanted to continue and tell her his plans. He was itching to tell her that he could see her in his future, standing side by side as the owners and bosses of a circus. Yet as she visibly seemed to shrink in her chair and bury her head behind the menu, he prudently decided to keep those thoughts to himself for the time being.

After dessert, Benjamín suggested a moonlight walk back to the circus. Melissa agreed. Walking hand in hand in muted companionship was meant to be calming for both of them, but Melissa was reprimanding herself for her behaviour in the restaurant. She was torn between what she wanted to say, what she wanted to happen, and what she was afraid *would* happen if she dared to open her heart.

Benjamín was also in turmoil. He thought he had found the woman he had been searching for his whole life, but now he wondered if his feelings would ever be reciprocated. It was due to their strained silence that Benjamín stopped and peered into the forest. "Did you hear that?"

"Hear what?"

"I think there's someone in the trees." He perused the forest, searching for a culprit but was met with total silence.

"Maybe it's an animal," Melissa suggested.

"Come out we can hear you..." he dropped her hand, waiting for someone to step out of the darkness and reveal themselves, but nothing happened.

Melissa shivered and pulled her thin, summer jacket closed across her chest. "You see, there's nobody there." She took his hand and walked to the caravan door. "Thank you for a lovely evening," she said and gave him a quick peck on the lips. As she turned away, Benjamin grabbed her wrist and pulled her to him. His arms folded around her, and he pulled her into a tight embrace. When he kissed her, Melissa's emotions exploded. His tongue explored her mouth, and she moaned with pleasure. When he pulled away, she wanted to grab him and beg for more.

This time he was the one to turn away. He gave her a mock salute. "See you tomorrow, Melissa." He grinned, turned his back and sauntered across the field into the night, leaving her aching with a need that only he could fulfil.

Thirty minutes later, Sarah crossed the field. She shivered as the night air penetrated her clothes and found her body still wet with sweat from her rehearsal on the web. She shuddered, yet she did not think it was just from the cold. As she neared the caravan, she had the distinct feeling of being watched. The hair on the back of her neck stood to attention. She stared intently into the nebulous gloom, the blackened night which, all of a sudden, seemed oppressive. Wispy tendrils of a cold breeze carried dusty leaves towards her, swirling like mini tornados rising from the forest floor. Unnerved, Sarah ran the remaining distance to the caravan, fumbled with her key, and continued to feel uneasy even when she was inside.

Her entrance caused little reaction to the three inhabitants. Melissa's love-struck expression was not lost on Sarah; neither were Wendy's rosy-hued cheeks from imbibing too much alcohol. Lisa's swollen eyes betrayed that she had been crying over Mario again. None of them were cognizant enough to acknowledge the fear that Sarah's highly distraught countenance exuded.

"I think there's someone outside in the trees."

That finally got a reaction.

Melissa sat bolt upright on the bed as fear and realisation got the better of her love-struck mood. "Benjamín said he thought he heard someone out there when we came back, but I couldn't see anyone."

Wendy also sat up straighter. "I thought I was being followed when we went to the mall today."

"What should we do?" Lisa looked from one girl to another in the hope of getting some sort of solution to their strange situation.

The four girls fell silent, lost for words. Sarah leaned across her bed towards one of the back windows. "Turn the lights off," she ordered to nobody in particular. When the van had been plunged into darkness, she peered through a chink in the flimsy curtains and peered out. into the blackened night. They were all at a height of nervousness that seemed to infect each other, the slightest movement inside or out of their flimsy home-made them jittery and bad-tempered.

"Well, if someone is watching us, I doubt we'd have much of a chance in this rust bucket. Anyone could break-in," Wendy announced. "All they'd have to do is jimmy the lock and I reckon they'd be in here in seconds!"

"Yeah, well thank you very much for that observation," Sarah's voice dripped with sarcasm, her eye still glued to the curtain while she perused the forest like a vigilant night watchman. A lone Screech-owl called out into the darkness, the chilling sound filled the sky and echoed into the night, making the girls jump in unison.

"But...who would be following you, Wendy?" Lisa's eyes had grown to twice their size. She stared at Wendy and the fear she was feeling was impossible to ignore.

"I think my husband might have sent someone to take me back home."

"It sounds a bit far-fetched to me," Melissa snorted, from drinking too much wine. "I mean; how would he even know that you came to Brazil?" She pondered on her statement for a minute. "If you'd run away to Brighton, or Blackpool I could understand it, but Brazil? It's like the other side of the world."

"Okay then," Wendy's frustration was obvious from her tone of voice. "If it's got nothing to do with me, let's hear your explanation as to why several people have now mentioned hearing or seeing something in the trees?"

Melissa's silence confirmed her lack of alacrity on the subject.

"It could be a Peeping Tom," Sarah said, her nose still glued to the curtains.

"Do you really think this could have something to do with your husband?" Lisa asked, her eyes growing even larger with every passing minute.

"He's a powerful man, Lisa," Wendy replied. "He has a lot of connections and a lot of people owe him favours. To be honest, I wouldn't put anything past him."

"Bloody hell!" Lisa interjected. "I'm not going to be able to sleep tonight!"

Sarah stepped away from the window. "I can't see anything. But, I do think we need to be vigilant. We shouldn't leave Wendy in here alone. We should stay together as a group or at least in pairs."

"Sarah's right," Melissa replied.

Wendy refrained from replying, realising that her coveted nights alone in the caravan had just disappeared quicker than Sienna's gloves and her crappy magic trick.

"Okay then, let's try and get some sleep. We've another busy day of rehearsals tomorrow," Sarah left her post at the curtains and wandered over to check the locked door and secure the windows. "Tomorrow we'll speak to Edwaldo. Maybe he can move our van to a different location."

Sleep was a long time coming that night – especially for Wendy. The owl screeched again and took flight swooping down to hook a mouse in its scissor-like talons. Nearby a tiny, yellow flame set alight a cigarette, the orange glow fizzing as its owner sucked nicotine into his lungs and waited.

∽

The next morning, the girls went to speak to Edwaldo. He listened to their tale, his face registering a look of sheer incredibility at both their story and their suggestion of repositioning the trailer. "Moving the caravan is an impossibility," he explained, with a slow shake of his head. "They are all strategically placed, it would be impossible to manoeuvre it out and even more impossible to place it further inside. Inconceivable." Concerned by their tired, frightened faces and dishevelled appearance, he decided to offer them a compromise. "I'll get one of the security men to stand guard behind your van, okay? That way you should at least be able to get some sleep."

He watched the girls visibly relax; tense shoulders dropped back to position, Wendy rubbed the back of her neck and they flashed weak smiles at one another, pleased that perhaps the presence of a man outside their caravan might help to keep intruders away. "Now, go prepare for rehearsals, we have a lot to accomplish today."

The morning passed quickly into the afternoon as the entire circus was put through their paces by Leonardo. The new show for Rio was beginning to take shape. Costumes were being made by a group of wives who were considered too old to perform but were still expected to help out. At Showtime, these same women contributed by selling popcorn, hamburgers, flashing lights, and other circus paraphernalia in the foyer tent before the show and during the interval. They presently sat at sewing machines which were hooked up to long extension cables beating time with the music as flashes of brightly coloured, sequined material and stretchy spandex passed under the whir of frenetic sewing needles.

For the day's rehearsal, the girls had come prepared. They had brought a selection of articles to keep themselves entertained when they were not rehearsing. Writing materials, magazines, and novels were devoured along with several snacks to keep up their energy and morale. Wendy, more than anyone else, was complacent, reticent, and bored with the entire proceedings. Her menial role in the entire magic extravaganza meant that she was forced to sit around for hours without doing a thing. At one point she even nodded off. She felt safe sitting in the tent and being surrounded by the entire circus cast. Lisa sat beside her, feeling strangely protective of her friend, but also more than a little sleepy herself. She jumped when a hand clasped her on the shoulder from behind. She spun around to see Mario smiling down at her.

"Lisa, we should talk. Come with me," he did not wait for confirmation before he sauntered off to the raised, tiered seating area and expecting her to follow him.

Lisa watched him go, torn between the loyalty for her friend and her attraction for a man from whom she felt unable to stay away. She glanced at Wendy whose head had dropped almost to her chest, steady breathing bordering on a snore rattled softly in her throat and landed on her light, cotton top causing it to fluctuate like a rippling tide across her chest.

Making a decision, Lisa stood up, pulled her leotard back into position and followed Mario. He sat down and patted the wooden seating board next to him. Lisa joined him, enjoying the tingling closeness of his body next to hers. He twisted to face her, his knee touching hers and making her insides tingle with sexual anticipation.

"Do you forgive me?" his puppy-dog eyes bored into Lisa's to such an extent her mouth lacked spittle. She ran a tongue across her dry lips. Mario followed its trajectory with lust in his eyes. "God, you are so beautiful," he made eye contact and watched Lisa almost melt under his smouldering gaze. "I'm sorry about the other day. It's just that you are so perfect, I can't bear to think of you with someone else. I want you only for me. And when I saw Edwaldo touching you..." he dropped his gaze and looked at his hands clasped together in his lap before looking into her eyes again. "I wanted to kill him."

Lisa listened to his outpour of sentiment and was overwhelmed by his emotion. She grasped his hands and stared into his eyes with an intensity that unnerved him.

"Mario, Edwaldo is married to Sienna, why would I want to be with him? You are the only man for me, but you need to understand that I have to talk to other people. That doesn't mean that I don't want to be with you, okay?"

Mario sighed, placated that she had believed his well-rehearsed speech. "Okay." With a theatrical glance left and right he slipped to the edge of the seat and stood. "Quick, come with me," he pulled her off the bench and began to stride to the end of the seating section.

Lisa giggled with the excitement of the situation. "Where are we going?"

"Behind here," Mario dragged her underneath the seating block and held her in a tight embrace. He kissed her with an intensity that, under normal circumstances, would have blown her mind, but when she spied the strategically placed acrobat crash mat laid on the floor, the magic was lost. She could not get the image of him and the call-girl out of her head.

Mario saw her falter. He dropped his hands. "That is not for you!" he said pointing at the offending mat that looked decidedly like a well-worn mattress. "You are too good to be taken on an old mat like some sordid little secret. When the time is right, then only the best for you, mi amor."

Placated, Lisa allowed him to kiss her again.

~

After a break for lunch, the members of the show were ordered back into the ring. Tempers were frayed as everyone was overworked, tired, and irritable. The stress of preparing for the important theatre production was taking its toll on everyone no matter how trivial their role in the proceedings.

The girls rehearsed their new routines under the scrutinising, ever-watchful eyes of Sienna and Lorenzo who were far from happy with anything that anyone did. Sienna barked orders left and right to anybody who would listen. Artists argued over-allocated ring times, new props were under construction, the entire tent was a hive of activity.

As the huge metal construction called 'The Wheel of Death' was hoisted up into position, the girls stood together pondering on what Sienna would find to shout about next. Miguel wandered over towards them. "Hi," he said while throwing three juggling balls into the air over and over again; catching them with one hand and a nonchalance that showed how relaxed and adept he was at his skill. "So, do you all feel ready for our big performance in Rio?" His question was addressed to them all, but whenever he took his eyes off the balls for a second, he only looked in Lisa's direction.

"No, not really," Melissa replied, wondering if he would even bother to acknowledge her existence, "and you?"

Miguel gave a short laugh, changed his one-handed trick to two and added a fourth ball. "Juggling on a stage rather than in a sawdust-covered ring is not very different for me," he admitted. "So, Lisa, have you ever thought about learning to juggle?" Lisa's demurred expression spurred him on. "Take the balls in one hand like this..."

The other three looked at one another with knowing smiles before casually walking away.

By four o'clock, Edwaldo called an end to rehearsals and told everyone to be back in an hour to start the show. As the girls left by the backstage door, Lisa saw Mario standing to one side. "Girls, you go on, I'll see you in a minute," she said, flashing them a love-struck smile. She tripped over towards him, her face beaming with happiness, but her smile slid from her face as she recognised the angry expression on his countenance.

"Are you playing with me?" he snarled, leaning towards her and invading her personal space.

Confused, Lisa took a step backwards. "What's wrong with you?"

"What's wrong with me?" his tone was one of incredulity. "What's wrong with you! You said I was the only man for you, then I turn my back for one minute, and you are with Miguel!"

Lisa shook her head in confusion, "He was teaching me to juggle in a tent full of people. How can there be anything wrong with that?"

Mario lashed out and slapped her hard across the face. "You are nothing but a whore!"

Lisa's hands flew to her face, feeling the heat from the slap turning her cheeks to flame-red. Tears coursed down her cheeks in humiliation. "I'm not a whore!" she shouted as Mario marched with defiant strides out of the tent. "I am NOT a whore!"

∼

In the caravan, after consoling Lisa, the girls tried to settle down to a meal, but the unmistakable raised voices of their arguing neighbours Philipe the clown and his wife Ariella were impossible to ignore. The girls did not hide their curiosity; their ears pricked towards the argument as they eavesdropped, even though they did not understand what was being said.

"What do you think they're arguing about?" Lisa glanced at each girl for some sort of confirmation.

"No idea," Wendy shrugged, "but it doesn't sound good."

Seconds later they heard the caravan door slam shut.

Sarah peeped behind the curtain, "Philipe has walked out."

They began to eat again, only to hear more raised voices, this time coming from the opposite line of trailers.

"That's Martina's voice," Lisa confirmed. "It sounds like she's not happy with her partner either."

"What's the matter with everyone this evening?" Melissa asked. "What with Mario and you, Lisa, Philipe and his missus, and now Martina and her other half. What the hell's got into everybody?"

"Maybe it's a full moon," Sara said from her peeping position behind the curtain. "Oh! The men are all getting together?"

"What do you mean?" Lisa ran to peep behind the other curtain to watch what was happening.

Wendy nodded her head as recognition struck. "I'll tell you exactly what's going on. These men have caused these arguments on purpose so that they can go out without having to explain to their other halves where they're going."

"Do you really think so?" Melissa looked doubtful.

Wendy forked more rice into her mouth without breaking her stride. "My husband used to do this all the time," she said, mid chomp. "He'd storm out of the house leaving me feeling that everything was my fault when it's just his means of escape."

"But why?" Lisa asked, intrigued by such a notion.

"Keep watching, Lisa, I bet you any money, they're all going to go to the girly bar across the street."

Lisa took Wendy's order literally. She threw on a jacket and left the caravan, slowly following the group of guys, now up to seven, including Edwaldo, Alfonso the driver, and Arturo the catcher from the flying trapeze.

"Uff! There'll be a lot of women with `mala leche´ tomorrow!" Wendy said, putting her knife and fork together and pushing her plate back with a contented sigh."That was a great meal, Melissa, thank you."

"Mala, leche? What's that supposed to mean?" Melissa stood up, removed both their plates from the little table, and put a pan on the stove to make coffee.

"A literal translation would be `bad milk´ but it's slang, so it sort of translates as `there'll be a lot of people in really bad moods tomorrow´."

"Oh, well that's just great!" Sarah said, pulling herself away from the curtain as Lisa's bent figure crept around the corner and out of sight. "We've got Sienna first thing in the morning for another bloody rehearsal!"

"Fabulous!" Wendy replied sarcastically and threw herself onto her bed, "I can't wait!"

Lisa followed the group until they entered the girly-bar. Her eyes stung as she thought of Mario meeting up with the call girl from the other night. Could it be possible that he had caused an argument so that he could go out? Or was she to blame? An errant tear caroused down her cheek and with one brusque swipe, she removed it. Should she stop talking to other male members of the circus? Would that please him? She could not remember seeing any other married females or girlfriends with partners talking to any other male - unless their other half was with them - or was she imagining it? If she was being honest with herself, she had not paid much attention. But the more she pondered, the more convinced she became that it was all her fault.

CHAPTER EIGHT

Ten o'clock the next morning, Wendy's prediction had come to fruition. Clusters of females stood in strategic points around the tent, whispering or muttering among themselves. With narrowed eyes, arms folded tightly across their chests and one foot strategically jutting out in front of them, they glared at their offending other halves with killer expressions. The men stood in little clusters, laughing and joking, cajoling each other in an over-exaggerated, outlandish, bravado-like fashion.

"Just look at them," Wendy tossed her head in the guys' direction. "That's the worst bit of acting I've seen in a while. They're trying to look macho and brave. They're sticking together to feel more confident because, deep down, they know that what they did last night was wrong."

"Bloody hell, you can cut the atmosphere in here with a knife!" Sarah commented.

Abruptly, the main doors to the tent crashed open and in stormed Sienna. Her hair fanning out behind her as she stomped towards the stage with long, purposeful strides in her bright yellow clogs. It was more than apparent to anyone who chose to glance in her direction that she was in a foul mood. She stood centre stage and perused her minions, ready to pounce on anyone who put the slightest foot wrong that morning.

Lorenzo was already sat in one of the ringside seats. He looked up and smiled in her direction, apparently oblivious to the killer atmosphere within the tent. He stood up, helped her enter the ring, then he climbed over the ring-fence and began fiddling with the CD player.

Sienna exhaled for various, long seconds to express her exasperation and to highlight the fact that she was running on an extremely short fuse. She clapped her hands. "Positions please, for the opening number." The girls and WAGs took their places behind both sets of side curtains and waited for the music to begin.

"STOP, STOP, STOP!" Sienna screamed after the first few bars of music bounced around the tent. She gabbled in a mixture of Brazilian and Italian to the offending WAG who had made a mistake. "AGAIN!" she screamed, and everyone slouched back behind the curtains.

"This is going to be a LONG day!" Wendy said with a sigh.

∼

During the first break, Benjamín came over to talk to Melissa. "What's the matter with everyone today? I hate this negative atmosphere."

"A group of the male artists went to the club across the road last night and most of their partners are not happy about it," Melissa replied, wondering how he could not have heard about the previous night's excursion when he had been interacting with the men all morning. She could never quite shake the feeling that he was constantly toying with her. He always seemed to be holding something back. Something that she should know, but for some reason, he was not telling her. Perhaps that's why she was playing it cool, not committing to the relationship, although she really wanted to.

Wendy's pep talks had also made her more reticent than she would perhaps have normally been.

"Oh, I see." He noticed the seriousness of her expression and wondered what she was thinking about. "Yes, that would account for it. So, Melissa, after the show shall we go out?"

Melissa gave him a small smile, more convinced than ever that his conversational starter had been a mere ruse. "Yeah, that would be nice," she said.

"Places everyone for the finale," Sienna bellowed and with resigned sighs, everyone complied.

Backstage, as they waited for the music to start, Fernando nudged Sarah, "How's the web going?"

"Okay," Sarah scrunched up her face to express her forthcoming apology. "Sorry I haven't been around much, but with the web and the magic rehearsals, I haven't had much free time to be able to practise the trapeze with you and your family." She looked away, feeling guilty for leading him on. She liked him as a person, he seemed like a good man, but she did not know if any feelings of romance would blossom on her part or not.

Fernando smiled. "I understand, don't worry. To be honest, we haven't had much time either. Arturo said that we should practise some new moves too, so we've also been pretty caught up in rehearsals."

"Oh, I'm glad about that," Sarah smiled, "I don't feel quite so bad now."

The music rattled through the aged speakers and Sarah made her excuses and shuffled into position.

Lisa risked a glance in Mario's direction. This time he made eye contact and smiled at her. Her heart flew to her mouth. She was unsure of how to interpret his actions. Was he making peace with her, or was his smile one of slyness, knowing what he had probably done last night. She decided to look away, her emotions in turmoil as the curtains opened and she dancing into the ring.

After the show, Sarah went straight into the tent with Melissa to practise the web. Benjamín would also be there and Fernando had invited himself too. Both girls needed someone to swing the ropes as they performed their moves at the top of the tent. Melissa had been hoping that Edwaldo would also put in an appearance. She wanted to tell him that his promised security guard had never appeared last night.

Lisa and Wendy were both in the caravan. Lisa lay prone on her bed contemplating her situation and trying to decipher Mario's smile. Wendy sat on the other bed writing a letter. She was fighting an inward struggle as the cravings for alcohol niggled at her taste buds, making her break out into a sweat. She needed to keep herself under control. She did not want the others to realise what she already knew, that her drinking was getting out of control.

Abruptly, Lisa stood up. "I'm going to go out for a walk. I can't stay in here all night."

Wendy looked up from her letter. "Okay, but don't waste your time on that loser, Mario, because, I'm telling you. He's a total waste of space."

Lisa gave her a curt nod but refrained from replying. Wendy's curt remark annoyed her. She did not want to admit to herself that, deep down, perhaps Wendy could be right. Was Mario just toying with her? Then she wondered if maybe Wendy was jealous of their relationship. Wendy had still not found a partner on the show, maybe she did not want to spend every night alone in the rust bucket and was trying to break them up. Despite her present situation, Lisa could not help the feelings she had for Mario. He was constantly in her thoughts, everything she did was with him in mind. She had to speak to him. Grabbing her thin jacket, she looked furtively in Wendy's direction. "I'm going out. See you later."

When Lisa left the van, Wendy shook her head, knowing that the girl would not listen to her. She thought back to her youth when she had never listened to her own mother. As she pondered on her past, a tiny pinprick of light shone through the curtain and she instinctively fell to the floor. Wendy heard the tread of heavy boots circling the caravan. Sliding under the bed as quietly as she possibly could, she held her breath. The intruder tried the door handle and jiggle the chain. Wendy placed a hand over her mouth to smother the sound of her errant breathing and exhaled with relief when she realised that Lisa had locked the door behind her when she left.

"Shit," she heard a male's muffled voice curse, followed by the same heavy tread as the man ran back into the safety of the trees. Seconds later, Wendy was up and shoving a few belongings into a bag. She pulled on her coat, pushed her feet into her boots and left the caravan as quietly as she possibly could. Heading in a straight line with the forest behind her, she hoped that the intruder would not pick up on the fact that she had escaped. Not knowing where she was going or when she would be back, she slipped away into the darkness.

Lisa completed her second lap of the circus, trying to build up the nerve to knock on Mario's parents' caravan again. She stood a few hundred yards away from their home staring at the door. In the gloom, she failed to notice Wendy veering sharply to the left and heading down towards the lake. Pondering her options, Lisa decided that if she was being honest, she had no idea if Mario was even on-site. She had tried his caravan. The lights were on, but for all she knew, he could be back at the girly bar again. "Come on," she silently chastised herself. "Just go over and knock on his parent's door."

Giving a sharp rap on the trailer, she stood there waiting. In her insecurity, she picked at a spot on her chin, then freaked out when she realised it was bleeding. The door opened as she was rubbing the blood from her face.

"Hola, ¿Está Mario aquí?"

His mum shook her head and peered towards Lisa.

"Estás sangrando..." she pointed towards Lisa's chin and the spot oozing blood.

"Yes, I know I'm bleeding! Is Mario here?" She swiped the wound with an angry swat of her hand.

"No, he go club," María pointed in the direction of the establishment whose distant music taunted Lisa as she imagined what was happening inside.

"Mario, bad boy," María's voice dropped to a whisper. "Bad for you," she waggled a swollen, crooked finger in front of Lisa's face. Lisa nodded and turned to go, pondering on her words. Was she really warning her to avoid her son, or was this a ruse to make Lisa stay away? She trudged back to the caravan deep in thought. She found the door wide open. Fernand and Benjamín were stood outside, waiting for Melissa and Sarah to add the final touches to their `going out´ attire.

"Where's Wendy?" Lisa asked, slightly unnerved by the fact that she was going to be alone in the caravan.

"No idea," Melissa jumped out of the van, followed by Sarah a couple of seconds later. "We're off out," Melissa continued.

"I'm sure she won't be long, wherever she is," Sarah replied. "Strange though, don't you think? I've never known her to ever go out at all unless she's with one of us."

Lisa nodded, "Very strange." She stared at the discarded letter lying on Wendy's bed.

~

The following morning the girls awoke en masse. Melissa stretched and yawned before pulling the covers back, crawling over Lisa and standing up. "Morning, everyone." Her cheery disposition warmed the hearts of the other two who both sat up and answered together.

"Morning."

"Where's Wendy? Didn't she come back last night?" Melissa stared at the empty side of her bed and immediately began to worry.

"Apparently not," Sarah replied.

"That's mega odd," Lisa got up and took a couple of steps closer to Wendy's bed as though she needed to see the evidence of her missing friend herself. "I bet it's got something to do with whoever has been sneaking around our caravan these last few nights."

"Do you think so?" Sarah also turned to look at the crumpled pillow where Wendy had been laying immediately after the show. "Maybe she got up earlier than the rest of us and went for a walk."

"What, without disturbing you? She'd have had to crawl right over the top of you."

Sarah considered her friend's statement. "Yeah, actually you're right. But, maybe I didn't feel her, I mean; we did drink rather a lot of wine last night, didn't we Melissa?"

Melissa gave an absent nod. "I think we'd better start looking for her or at least tell someone. I mean; anything could have happened."

Foregoing breakfast they pulled on their clothes and headed out in search of Wendy. An hour later, tired and hungry, they headed back to the circus and sought the help of several artists. Before long, most of the show was out looking for her.

"Should we split up, do you think?" Lisa's doleful eyes sought out a reply. "We could cover more ground if we did that.

"That's correct," Melissa agreed, "but if it's true, and the person in the woods isn't just targeting Wendy and is after any one of us, we're giving him a fantastic opportunity. I think we should stick together."

"What if she went to the lake?" Lisa replied. "She said it was really beautiful down there, do you remember?"

"That's true," Sarah nodded. "Let's try there then." They set off in the general direction until they heard a familiar voice.

"Lisa, where you go?"

Lisa recognised the voice and stiffened. She did not turn around.

"It's Mario," Sarah mumbled, "are you going to speak to him?"

"No." Lisa was still angry with him. She could not stop thinking about the club and what he had probably been doing the previous night. She set off walking across the field, stepping out with elongated, gigantic strides to get as far away from him as she possibly could.

Sarah swung around to face Mario. "Sorry," she said, her voice lowered. "I don't think she wants to talk to you."

Mario shoved his hands in his pockets and shrugged. "Okay, I speak to her later," he said.

"We can't find Wendy; we are searching for her. Can you help?"

Mario stood and stared at her for a few seconds, his piercing eyes assessing both her and the situation.

"I will go this way," he said and headed back in the direction of the site.

"Thanks!" Sarah called after him. Seriously doubting that he would do anything.

∽

Down by the riverside, the girls scanned the area for any sign of their lost friend.

Lisa looked out into the middle of the water. "You don't think she would have done something stupid, do you? You don't think she's tried to kill herself?"

"Nah," Sarah replied, her vocalisation didn't quite match her facial expression which openly showed her concern. "She's got to be around here somewhere."

"Yeah, but she's drinking way too much. She could have lost her footing and fallen into the river," Melissa replied. "I hope not, but it could have happened."

Lisa cupped her hands to her mouth and shouted: "WENDY!"

The other two followed suit. "WENDY!"

Melissa spun around. "Look!"

Wendy came shuffling towards them. She was dripping wet and covered in mud, so much so, that her shoes no longer resembled footwear. The sticky substance clung to her legs as though she were wearing some sort of seventies knee socks. Detritus from the riverbank held fast in her hair, making her look like some weird looking scarecrow.

"What the hell happened?" Sarah looked at her friend's dishevelled appearance in horror.

"Don't worry, I'll be fine!" Wendy wafted two hands up and down in an attempt to calm them down and to stop any more questions.

"But, what happened?" Lisa's exasperation forced Wendy to reply.

After explaining about the strange light and someone trying the door, she told them how she had thrown a few things into a bag and left.

"But, look at the state of you!" Melissa exclaimed. "Where have you been?"

"I managed to come down here, and I found a hollowed-out tree, so I tipped it upside down and slept underneath it, rather like an overturned boat."

"Cool!" Lisa replied, thinking how inventive her friend was under such frightening circumstances.

"Okay, but that doesn't explain the mud," Melissa replied.

"Well, actually that's the silly part. I got up this morning and thought that I must look a sight, so I decided to wash my face and hands in the river before I set off back for the circus."

"Yeah, and?" Lisa urged.

"Well," Wendy gave an embarrassed smile, "the river bank was so slippery, I fell in!"

Lisa guffawed with laughter, her giggling became infectious and set off the other three. They silently acknowledged that their laughter was partly from relief at finding their friend.

"Just look at the state of you!" Sarah screeched, pointing at the dishevelled mess before her.

"Come on, let's get back to the circus. We've got a lot of explaining to do." Melissa shook her head at Wendy's predicament and began walking out of the park. "I'm glad you're okay though."

"Thanks," Wendy replied. "I just hope it doesn't happen again."

"It's our last night here," Sarah reminded them. "As long as we all stick together, I'm sure we'll be fine."

By the end of the second show, the girls had already packed down their caravan, the cupboard doors were tied together with string, the caravan legs had been wrenched up, the electric cable and water pipes had been rolled and stored, and the gas bottle sat in the middle of the floor. The girls hung around their van, waiting impatiently for Alfonso's arrival. When they saw him striding towards them, they held out their hands in mock fashion, showing him how prepared they were to leave at the first available opportunity.

Alfonso stopped short with his hands on his hips and shook his head. "Wow! I'm impressed," he said as the girls grinned in unison. "But, I'm sorry, you will have to wait until the last. I have my orders." He felt uncomfortable when he saw their smiles disappear quicker than kids out of a classroom. When there was no reply, he turned away and sauntered towards the next caravan.

"Well, that's just great!" Wendy replied. "If we're left until last, whoever is in the woods will have the perfect opportunity to approach us."

"Maybe," Melissa replied, "but maybe not. If he knows that everyone is moving, it makes sense that he would move too. If he has no idea where the show is going, then the earlier he leaves, the sooner he can find accommodation. But if he stays until the early hours of the morning, he'll have a much harder time."

"Melissa's got a point, Wendy. Also, he doesn't know that we're usually left until the very end. I mean; these strange occurrences have only begun to happen here," Sarah said.

Wendy nodded. "Perhaps you're right, but maybe we've only become aware of his existence here. He could have been following us for weeks."

"I doubt it," Lisa replied.

"Well, I'm still going to sit out here with a bloody big knife in my hand," Wendy pledged.

"Okay, okay," Sarah said, hoping to calm Wendy down, yet

thinking that perhaps they should all consider sitting with knives in their hands. "So, if we've got to stay until the end, we might as well make the most of it. Lisa, get the portable barbeque out, Melissa get the wine and let's have a party!"

With the help of the Chinese, Alfonso had just finished hoisting their caravan onto the tow-bar when he became aware of the sudden activity around the girls' van. He smiled to himself and shook his head when he saw the barbeque being carried outside along with a host of fold-up chairs. *Those girls sure know how to party,* he thought.

As the hours rolled by and there was no sign of any intruder, Wendy began to relax. The wine flowed, and the girls began to open up and talk about their secrets and fears.

"What makes you think that the intruder is specifically after you?" Lisa asked Wendy. "He could be some wierdo stalker who would be quite happy to see anyone of us in some stage of undress."

"Don't you remember what Wendy said?" Sarah replied. "Her husband is dangerous; he could have hired someone to find out where she is, to take her back to the UK."

"Or worse," Wendy drained the bottom of her glass. "He could have hired someone to kill me."

Melissa drew in a long frightened breath, "You don't really think he'd do that, do you?"

Wendy shrugged and beckoned Lisa to top up her glass. "With my husband, I think anything is possible."

"Bloody hell!" Lisa shivered and pulled her jacket closed across her chest.

"Anyway, never mind me," Wendy said, changing the conversation and throwing Lisa into the spotlight. "What's going on with you and Mario? It seems to me it's on again and off again more times than the blinking neon sign at the club over the road."

Lisa squirmed in her seat, "I dunno." She lowered her eyes, hoping Wendy would move on to someone else.

"I've told you, he's no good for you. But you won't listen."

"His mother told me too, yesterday."

"Well, there you go then," Wendy turned her attention to Sarah. "And what's happening with you? How's the..." she held up her fingers to imitate inverted commas. "Fernando affair?"

"Well, it's sort of been a bit on the back burner. I've been so tied up with rehearsals for the magic and the web that I haven't had much chance to practise the trapeze. And anyway, he said he's also been busy because his family is practising new tricks for the theatre show."

Wendy scrutinised Sarah's facial expressions. "If you ask me, you're not overly into this guy are you?"

Sarah sighed. "I'm going to tell you all something which I have only told my family."

The three girls shuffled to the edge of their seats. Intrigued to hear what she was about to divulge.

"I only took this job because I had a huge argument with my parents."

"What about?" Lisa's eyes sparkled from the barbeque coals as she sipped her wine and waited with anticipation for an answer.

"It's all a bit embarrassing, to be honest," she squirmed in her seat. "But, to cut a long story short, my parents came home earlier than I was expecting and they caught me in bed with a woman."

"Shit!" Lisa jumped and almost spilled her wine. "You mean to tell me you're gay?"

Sarah looked around the group. "To be honest, I think I'm bisexual, I think. Well. I must be, I like both sexes."

"That makes a lot of sense," Wendy said. "I've seen the way you watch Sienna move around the ring. I did wonder."

Lisa's face showed her abhorrence. "Sienna? No way!"

Sarah shrugged, "Ah, come on, Lisa, you've got to admit that she's attractive!"

Lisa considered for a few seconds then shrugged and smiled.

"So, what happened with your parents?" Melissa asked.

"They were appalled. Dad in particular. He wouldn't let me explain. He told me to get out and to never come back."

"That's a bit extreme," Lisa replied.

"So, what's your plan? I mean, what will you do at the end of this contract?" Wendy asked.

"I don't know. Hopefully, find another one beforehand. If not, I'm up shit creek without a paddle as they say."

The four girls fell silent, pondering on the situation. Then Wendy spoke:

"And now we come to our very own lovesick Melissa, what are you going to do?"

Now it was Melissa's turn to sigh. "I don't know, I like him an awful lot, but I can't help it, I always feel like he's playing with me."

"How do you mean?"

"I don't exactly know, but, sometimes I think he's laughing at me as if there's more to his story than he's prepared to tell me."

"Like what?" Lisa swirled the wine around her glass and waited for an answer.

"I don't know; maybe he's married or something and just stringing me along."

"I find that a little hard to believe," Wendy said. "I've seen the way he looks at you, he's smitten, I'd say."

"I agree," Sarah concurred.

"Me too," Lisa nodded.

Melissa stared off into the distance looking pensive.

Wendy's heart skipped a beat. "What's the matter?" Her hand grabbed for the kitchen knife she had recently discarded by her feet. Her head spun from left to right, scanning the area. "Have you seen someone?"

"No," Melissa replied absently.

Wendy relaxed again and took a good swig of her wine.

"Maybe I'm being over-cautious. My last relationship finished exactly for that reason. I found out the guy was married. But, it's not just that; I can't help but think about other things, you know, like... would I want to spend the rest of my life in a circus? All this upheaval every couple of weeks or sometimes even shorter. It must get annoying."

"You've got a point there," Sarah concurred, "I mean, I hate the thought of it now, and we've only been doing it for two minutes!"

Lisa laughed.

Melissa did not. She was still lost in her thoughts. "Then I think, do I want to spend the rest of my life swanning around in a caravan?"

"You could be the next Sienna!" Wendy's sarcastic grin made Lisa and Sarah smile. Melissa remained lost in her thoughts.

"I guess only time will tell," she said, finishing with a melancholic sigh.

CHAPTER NINE

In the early hours of the morning, the girls were driven to an abandoned plot in the vicinity of the Metropolitan Theatre in Rio de Janeiro. They had hoped that, as they were not working in the tent, they would be able to have a bit of a lie-in, but it was not to be. Martina had woken them up at eight o'clock, to tell them that they would be expected to be at the front of the circus in approximately half an hour because the whole show was going to rehearse in the theatre.

The four girls grumbled at their lack of sleep but they were also excited. For dancers, the thrill, ambience, and pure aesthetic beauty of a theatre is the pivotal point for them.

"I've never worked in a theatre," Lisa confessed. "What's it like?" Her jitteriness, due to her excitement, was addictive and the other girls regaled her with stories of their past experiences.

"It's just such a magical feeling," Melissa began. "How can I explain it?... It's the sheer pleasure of stepping into the auditorium, with its high ceilings, balconies, galleries, the dress circle, the gods, it's an amazing experience."

Wendy nodded in agreement. "You feel as though you've stepped back in time to an era when opulence was the forte, where only the rich could attend such places."

"And there's a certain smell to everything, unlike anywhere else in the world. And the feel of the plush velvet seating makes you feel as though you are connecting with artists from the past and present that have performed there," Sarah explained.

"That's true," Melissa confirmed. "There's a stillness to an empty theatre that exudes shivers of energy as though ghostly actors walk the boards whenever they feel like it. And if it's an older theatre, the dressing-rooms are always in the bowels of the building and are usually deathly cold."

"That's so true!" Wendy agreed. "And usually they emit a musty, earth-like odour that makes those more sensitive amongst us prefer not to venture down there alone."

"Okay, guys, that's enough. You're beginning to freak me out now!" Lisa complained.

When the van pulled up outside the building, Lisa could hardly wait to get inside the theatre. She skipped to the door urging the others to hurry up. They went through the foyer into the auditorium and Lisa came to a complete standstill. the expanse of the theatre caused her mouth to hang open in pure astonishment. The front curtains had been raised and the sheer size of the enormous stage made her shake her head in wonder.

"Stop catching flies!" Wendy gave her a gentle push on her shoulder. "Now, come on."

The girls wandered around the stage which was alive with activity as the artists swung from ropes testing the rigging and hanging their trapeze equipment, the wheel of death, the webs, and other aerial acts. Other guys were in the process of rebuilding their equipment in the wings and huge backstage area. The Globe of Death was riveted together section by section like piecing together a huge orange, while one member of the group tested the four motorbikes that would ride around it in formation. Billows of grey smoke and the acrid smell of diesel burning hit the backs of their throats as he revved the bikes to their full capacity.

Sienna appeared from behind one of the many illusions that Edwaldo and his ring boys were unpacking and putting together. "Oh, here you are. Come with me. I will show you your dressing room."

The girls tripped after her and came to one of three doors marked `Ballerinas´. Theirs was to be the third room, and they would not have to share it with the rest of the WAGs.

Stepping inside, they immediately chose their spot in front of four lighted mirrors. Lisa walked around the small room, touching everything like an awestruck fan. She even touched one of the bright lightbulbs around the mirrors and flinched when the heat burnt her fingers.

"At least the dressing-rooms are on the same level as the stage. I won't feel too frightened to stay in here on my own." Wendy said.

"That's true," Melissa agreed.

Sienna broke into their train of thought. "Okay, you've got half an hour to find your costumes and to prepare them. Then, come to the stage. We are going to do a complete run-through of the new show."

"Okay," Sarah replied for them all, then when Sienna left the room, she whispered: "Another fun-filled day of marching around the stage and dancing mundane routines that a six-year-old could do."

Half an hour later, the girls stood in their opening costumes, waiting for the stage to clear. They hung around immersed in the strange, atmospheric mix of theatre and circus. Lisa still looked star-struck. Her eyes perused every part of the enormous theatre from the lighting rigs above her to the orchestra pit at her feet with an enormous grin across her face.

Benjamín, also dressed in his Ringmaster's uniform, wended over towards Melissa and slipped his arm around her waist. "Hello!" For once his sultry tone was lost on Melissa as she analysed every aspect of the theatre.

"It's magnificent, isn't it?" she replied, barely glancing in his direction.

"What is magnificent? You or the theatre?" He did not wait for a reply. "Because, if I had to choose I would pick you."

Melissa grinned and tapped him on his chest. "Don't be silly!" Her laughter was cut short when he leaned in with an abruptness that startled her and planted a passionate kiss on her lips. Melissa was elated by his emotion, but she felt herself redden. Other than the girls, she could not remember him ever openly expressing his desire in front of the other members of the circus before. She scanned the stage to see several members nudging each other, laughing and whispering to themselves. She was not entirely sure how she felt about it. Their secret was well and truly out. If she was part of some furtive scheme, and he was hiding a clandestine wife somewhere in the shadows, then his other half would almost certainly find out about them now. She looked across at Sarah who gave her a crafty smile that expressed her pleasure at their show of emotion. Then, in a flash, the moment was lost as Sienna clapped her hands together from the front of the stage and ordered everyone to be ready to begin in one minute. The Jets and the Sharks grabbed the drums and drumsticks and hoisted the weighty instruments onto their shoulder with the thick strap. They secured the heavy, furry beefeater style hats into position under their chins and took their places at either side of the stage.

By two o'clock they had completed the first run through. There had been a few minor hitches, but all in all, it had gone well. Edwaldo pointed to a long table set up in the auditorium. It was laden with burgers, pizzas, fries, and a few other dishes. "Well done, everyone," he said, applauding them all. The clapping elevated as everyone joined in, pleased that everything had gone well. The applause ricocheted around the theatre and Lisa, being in the moment, performed a theatrical bow.

"Everyone, please eat," Edwaldo said. "At three-thirty, we will be doing a parade through the centre of Rio. Sienna will instruct you all and tell you what costumes you should wear. Please make sure that you are in the foyer of the theatre by three fifteen."

There was a mad rush for the food. Everyone was hungry and the thought of doing a parade, which according to Wendy could last at least two hours, made the girls want to stock up on carbohydrates to keep their energy levels up.

They grabbed what they could - without looking like they were raiding a pantry - and scuffled back to their dressing-room with their goodies. Sienna was there when they stepped inside. She held up four `all-in-one's´ a leotard and tights cut from one piece of cloth and stitched together rather like a baby-grow or jumpsuit. They were in four different colours with sections cut out down the arms, stomach, and legs. On the table were four feather headdresses of matching colours.

"Ah, here you are," she eyed their abundance of food but refrained from commenting. The girls put their alimentary stash down on the nearest free surface, feeling somewhat guilty for having an appetite. "These are the costumes I want you to wear for the parade."

Wendy screwed up her nose at the design of the suits. She lifted her chin and rolled her eyes to the ceiling in silent disgust.

"What's the protocol?" Melissa asked, biting into her hamburger. "I mean; how do we do this parade? Do we have to walk down the streets or what?"

It was Sienna's turn to cast her eyes heavenwards to show her annoyance. "There will be an open-topped bus. Everyone will be positioned on the first or second floor."

"Let's hope we can stay on the first floor and sit down to hide those hideous efforts of so-called costumes," Wendy muttered as Sienna strode out of their dressing-room.

"Why what's wrong with them?" Lisa asked.

Wendy laughed at her naivety. "I guess this means that we'll have to dance at the side of Princess Sienna."

"What makes you say that?" Melissa picked up one of the costumes and analysed it.

"Because of these costumes! Look at the cut-out sections."

"What about them?"

"The majority of the cut-outs are at our knees, hips, and stomach," Wendy pointed a finger in an accusatory fashion towards the costumes' holes. "I'd like to bet you any money that Sienna will have one of her Gucci style costumes on and we'll look like the scrags of the litter in these abominations."

Lisa grabbed the pink costume and pulled it on. She stared with disbelief at her image in the mirror. "Oh, for fuck's sake!" she said. "I look like I've just been poorly made in the sausage factory!" She was hardly overweight, but the strategically placed holes accentuated all the wrong parts of a woman's body.

The others laughed at how ridiculous she looked. Lisa, unperturbed sobered them up with one single comment. "And, so will you!"

Half an hour later, kitted out in their disgusting costumes, they made their way to the bus feeling extremely ridiculous. To make matters worse, the WAGs were tittering together in their much more conservative costumes.

"I could kill bloody Sienna, the stupid bitch!" Lisa scowled as they shuffled past the rest of the artists who all had a gander and a giggle at their expense.

To Wendy's dismay, she found that the bottom deck of the bus was also open and she let out a groan. "Bloody hell, I don't know what is worse; to be on the bottom or the top of the bloody bus!"

Sienna stood by the vehicle, shouting orders at everyone and telling them exactly where to stand. She wore a dressing-gown which covered her costume, but just by looking at her tights and sparkling high heeled shoes, the girls knew that underneath the robe was a stunning ensemble.

Wendy was proven correct when Sienna eventually joined them at the top of the bus. All the other dancers had been relegated to the bottom deck, and only a handful of the better-looking males were given a position at the top with the Princess.

A speaker system had been rigged up at the front of the top deck. The sound system guy fiddled with knobs and buttons until the show music blared out at an alarming volume, with the booming voice of Edwaldo advertising the show. The bus lurched forwards and the girls grabbed the handrails to stop themselves from falling over the sides. Sienna glared at them, despite the fact that she had also taken hold of the handrail. "Dance, dance!" she snapped. When the bus set off again at a more constant pace, the girls tried their best to move in time to the music while Sienna kept a tight hold of the rail with one hand and waved at the crowds of unsuspecting passers-by with the other.

"Just look at her," Melissa seethed. "She thinks she's the Queen of bloody England!"

"What does that make you then?" Wendy quipped. "Princess Anne?"

Sienna gave a tut and glared at the giggling girls. "Dance!"

The bus veered down a side street and the sound system guy turned and shouted to those on the top deck.

"Tened cuidado con los cables!"

"What did he say?" Lisa turned to look at the others, her facial expression was one of annoyance and frustration. Unfortunately, she was facing away from the front of the bus and did not react quickly enough. The girls saw the other members squat down to the floor as a string of thick, dirty, black cables swung across the road from one building to the other. They smashed into the back of Lisa's head. As she turned around to see what had happened, the cables slid across her face, smearing her with years of dust and grime. She yelped. Both hands flew to cover her face as the bus continued on its wobbly journey. When the others finally stood up, Lisa had been rubbing her face in a vain attempt at removing the grime. When she dropped her hands, the others could not help it. They burst into laughter.

"Bloody hell, Lisa!" Wendy chuckled. "You might have looked like a mismade sausage before, but now, you look like one that's moonlighting as a chimney sweep!"

Sarah and Melissa screamed with laughter, but Lisa was almost in tears.

"Well, that's your new phrase for the day," Melissa giggled.

Lisa frowned, "What is?"

Melissa shook her head, "`Tened cuidado con los cables´. It means `be careful of the cables´!"

Two hours later, the bus pulled up outside the theatre. Lisa could not get off the bus quickly enough. She wanted to get to the dressing-room without being seen. Walking with her head down, hoping not to make eye contact with anyone, she pushed past those who had already left the bus and hurtled inside the theatre.

"Lisa, what happened?" Mario's voice rang out across the foyer.

Lisa stopped momentarily, unsure whether to ignore him or answer him. Either way, she did not want him to see her in this state. She cast her eyes in his direction. He saw her smeared visage and came running over to her. When he took her face in his hands, her eyes almost overflowed with unshed tears. He saw her discomfort and said: "Come with me."

Lisa was bustled into his dressing-room where she found that, fortunately, his family members had still not arrived back from the bus. He cleaned her face with water from the small washbasin and a new washcloth positioned on the side. As her tears finally fell, she knew they were not only because of the cables but because of the uncertain predicament she now found herself in with Mario. He saw her discomfort and held her in a tight embrace. "Don't cry, Bonita. Everything will be okay." He bent her head towards him and gently kissed each eye. Then, before she knew it, they were kissing in a passionate embrace. Her resolve to stay away from him dissipated as every living cell of her body yearned for him.

A hesitant cough in the doorway interrupted their embrace. They pulled apart to find Mario's father standing with his arms crossed and a satisfied smirk on his face.

"Vaya, vaya vaya!" he grinned as he walked into the room and sat down.

"What?" Lisa asked, the familiar feeling of discomfort at not understanding the language niggled at her conscience and left her feeling like an outsider.

"Nothing," Mario dismissed it. "Are you okay now?"

"Yes..." her voice sounded hesitant and unsure.

"Okay then. Go back to your dressing-room and get ready for the show. I'll see you afterwards, okay?" He squeezed her elbow and deftly manoeuvred her to the doorway. Then he lightly pushed her through. "Buena Suerte! That means 'Good Luck'," he grinned.

Lisa gave him her most radiant smile and almost skipped back to her dressing-room.

~

The show that evening was a grand affair. The Theatre was heaving with clientele who had paid handsomely to attend. The general hustle and bustle as the excited theatregoers searched for their seats and the gentle murmuring as they conversed with family and friends gradually grew in volume to a loud, excited chatter. Even the warm-up strains of musical rifts and chords from the orchestra in the pit were almost drowned out by the noise. The front of the auditorium held tables and chairs where the audience could dine while watching the circus show. These had been reserved months in advance by the crème de la crème of Rio's society. They sat in their refinery; the men smoking thick cigars and flashing Rolex watches and thick gold chains. The women wearing sleek evening dresses that clung to their slim figures. Their hands, ears, and throats glittering with jewels sparkling like moonlight on the ocean.

Edwaldo paced the stage behind the front curtains, his anxiety more than evident by his body language and nervous gait. He sent the ring boys scurrying in different directions as he made last-minute changes to the positioning of props, lights, and anything else his eyes happened to fall upon.

The girls looked around at the host of different activities backstage, the acrobats practising their tumbling, the trapeze group patting their hands with resin and binding their wrists with tape. The contortionist was already bent double on her red, sparkling podium. Her chest on the base, her spine doubled over so that her behind almost rested on the top of her head. Her feet were tucked under her chin while she chatted to her trainer. Her nonchalance implied that despite everyone else viewing her unusual position as out of the ordinary, it was, in fact, a perfectly normal and everyday occurrence for her.

"Two minutes to curtain," one of the backstage theatre-hands announced, and the girls surged towards the drums stacked up on a side table.

"Here we go then, break a leg," Melissa said, glancing at the others before they separated and took their positions in the wings, at either side of the stage.

"Buena Suerte," Lisa said with a shy smile in the WAG's direction. "That means ʻGood Luckʼ," she informed the others.

"Wow!" Wendy exclaimed, "A few more weeks and you'll be fluent." Her sarcasm was lost on Lisa who grinned with delight.

The first chords of the overture rose from the orchestra pit; a haunting sound exuding excitement, and the promise of future thrills. As the music reverberated around the theatre, the audience shuffled in their seats with excited anticipation. The performers wet their dry lips, tried to still those intrepid butterflies that swirled like mini tornados in some of their stomachs, and they focused on the task ahead.

The heavy, thick, red, velvet curtains slowly parted and the amalgam of dancing girls entered diagonally from left and right, filling the stage with their marching and drumming...

Backstage after the show, the energy was electric. The show had been almost flawless in its execution, and everyone was ready to party. The girls stood in the doorway of their dressing-room watching Edwaldo. He walked around the backstage with a permanent, broad grin etched on his face. Some of Rio's most elite members accompanied him as he ambled from artist to artist, introducing his guests to them and patting his artists' shoulders or backs with emphatic slaps. He grabbed veteran performers by their faces as though they were old lovers and planted a kiss on each cheek.

"Someone's happy," Wendy said, looking in his direction.

"I'm not!" Lisa grumbled, attempting to dry her hair with a small hand towel. "If I'd known that I was going to get soaked to the skin every night doing that bloody illusion, I would have refused to do it!"

"What did you expect? The trick's called the water illusion... Durr!" Wendy replied.

Miffed, Lisa bent forward so her long blonde hair flopped in front of her face and continued rubbing it with angry buffs so she would not have to reply.

When a pair of dark blue clogs came to a stop in her periphery, she slowly stood erect, following the line of the masculine legs, still clad in dark blue lycra, to his hands clutching his juggling clubs which, for once, were inactive. Her eyes continued upwards to the puffy, floating chemise type top, dotted with sequins and droplets, up to the nape of his neck until she found his smiling face.

"Hola Miguel," she said, glancing around frantically for any sign of Mario.

He could tell she was agitated by his presence. "Don't worry, I won't stay long. I just wanted to congratulate you on your excellent performance on the water illusion. It looked absolutely fantastic!" His perfect smile, made her feel warm inside but this sentiment was marred by the thought of Mario catching the two of them together.

"Thank you," she smiled, then grabbed her wet hair again. "But look at my hair! That trick is going to ruin it."

"Nonsense! You look very beautiful."

There followed an uncomfortable, pregnant pause while both of them were momentarily lost for words. Miguel recovered first. "Anyway, I better get going," he clicked the heels of his clogs together, like a German soldier and sauntered into the middle of the partying crowd.

Wendy, who had witnessed the whole encounter felt impelled to comment. "Now, he is a good man," she said, pointing an accusatory finger in Lisa's direction. "And he is crazy about you. So, now, it's your decision." She crossed her arms and walked closer to Lisa. "To be honest, I find this whole scenario fascinating. You've got a good guy and a bad guy on either shoulder and it's decision time. Who are you going to choose? Bad boy Mario, who will dump you as soon as another new bit of skirt comes along, or Miguel, who seems gentle and kind – hell, he seems too good to be true. But he won't wait around forever."

Lisa glared at Wendy, walked into the dressing-room, and threw the towel into the sink. *What does she know!* Lisa thought. A niggling voice was telling her that Wendy was probably right, but Lisa was not ready to heed the warning.

Waiting for Lisa to finish drying her hair, Melissa, Sarah, and Wendy remained on the periphery of the celebration, unsure whether to join in or wait to be asked. As they contemplated what to do, Sienna came sauntering past. She ignored Wendy and cast such a scathing look in Melissa and Sarah's direction that Melissa grabbed Sarah's arm. "What the hell is up with her?"

"God only knows!"

"I'll tell you what's up with her," Wendy replied. "You two have seriously pissed her off."

"Why?"

"How?"

Wendy shook her head in mock bewilderment. "Honestly, you two! How can you not know?"

The girls looked at each other for some sign of recognition but shook their heads.

"What?" Melissa pushed.

"It's your magic trick with the tiger."

"What about it?" Sarah sighed and put a hand on her hip, readying herself for whatever Wendy was about to disclose.

"From the second you walked on stage in those tiger skin, lycra leotards, and your silver high heels, there was a never-ending supply of wolf whistles..."

"Yeah, and?" Sarah's face registered her bewilderment as to where the conversation was going.

"Well, at the end of the trick when you came out of the cage, the wolf-whistling started up again, didn't it?"

"So what?" Melissa threw her hands up towards the ceiling. "What's your point? I don't get it."

"Neither does Sienna," Wendy replied. "Who follows the tiger trick?" She did not wait for an answer. "I'll tell you who; Sienna that's who. And who didn't get as many wolf whistles as you two?"

"Ahh!" the girls said in unison.

"So, Princess Sienna is not a happy camper."

Their eyes returned to the celebrations and were just in time to see a tall, slim woman with long, flowing, curly, black hair come sauntering onto the stage. Sienna made a big deal out of welcoming her, hugging her and kissing her.

The girls continued to stare when Benjamín held both his arms open and the newcomer ran towards him. Melissa's heart skipped a beat. She watched as the woman curled her arms around Benjamín's neck and he pulled her close.

"Ooh! What's going on here? Melissa, I think you've got competition," Wendy said, maliciously.

Melissa ignored her. She felt stripped of all feeling. How could this be happening to her again?

"Who is that?" Sarah took a sip of her drink and watched the interaction from the brim of her plastic cup.

Melissa's mind was working tenfold. It seemed that she had been right all along. This woman must be his wife. Benjamín put an arm around the woman's waist and escorted her over to the table to get her a drink and try to salvage a bit of food from the meagre remains. They laughed and talked together with an easiness that accentuated their familiarity with one another. Melissa felt sick. All this time he had been stringing her along when he had a wife. *How could he do this to me?* she inwardly screamed. She could not believe that history was repeating itself and she had fallen for a married man a second time. "It's got to be his wife," she blurted out with an anger that surprised even herself. "It stands to reason that she would come today when it's the opening night in such an important place."

"It could be just a friend," Sarah said, trying to convince her or at least give her a little bit of hope.

"No, I always knew he was hiding something from me. Now I know for sure."

Benjamín suddenly made eye contact and beckoned her towards him.

Melissa shook herself slightly, held her head up high, and walked back into the dressing-room. She had no desire to become embroiled in a sordid love triangle. A threesome where she held the minority role was not her thing. She was only happy that she had not given herself to him or she would have felt even worse than she did at the moment.

By the end of the party, several inebriated artists staggered around backstage with their significant other halves, each trying to hold the other upright. Others were passed out in the dressing-rooms. The driver, Alfonso seemed to have disappeared, and the girls concluded that they were probably going to have to crash on the dressing-room floor. None of them knew the address of the circus site - even if they had the slightest idea how to catch a cab.

As three of them threw towels and clothes on the floor to form some semblance of a bed, Sarah asked:

"Where's Lisa?"

"I saw her walking off with Mario," Wendy replied. "He's bad news. She should stay away from him. I've tried to warn her, but will she listen? No!"

"Well, let's try and get some shut-eye," Melissa replied. "I hope they let us go home in the morning so we can have a shower and something to eat. I don't want to live in the bloody theatre, no matter how lovely it is."

Backstage, in the darkest corner, Mario and Lisa lay on the crash mat. He slept with one arm draped protectively across her waist; his mouth hung slightly open and a series of light snores filled Lisa's ears. She could not sleep, tears rolled down her face. She was ashamed of herself, she had allowed Mario to take her. She had wanted to please him and had given herself to him on the same crashmat she had seen him fondling the call girl from the last town. Now, she swiped the endless tears from her face, the mascara mingling with the remains of her show make-up, forming a mottled design depicting, heartache, deception, and hurt pride. She wondered if Mario had even realised that he had just deflowered a virgin. She doubted it. He had shown no tenderness in his approach. She had told him that she was nervous, but he had brushed her feelings aside. He had made her feel that if she did not show him how much she loved him, she would lose him forever. Now she lay in a small puddle of blood, ashamed of her alcohol-infused actions and afraid to move in case Mario lost his temper.

CHAPTER TEN

SINCE THE PARTY two weeks ago, the girls had become a secular unit. Melissa and Lisa felt there was safety in numbers and were hiding away from their other halves – for want of a better word. Melissa was adamant that her relationship was well and truly over whereas Lisa did not feel particularly sure that hers was still ongoing. Sarah hung around as she had nothing better to do while Wendy secretly wished that they would all bugger off so that she could have some much needed alone time.

There was a nip in the air that evening and the girls had decided to partake of an alcoholic beverage... or two ...or three from the cosy if somewhat cramped confines of their tiny caravan.

"So, what's the situation with Benjamín?" Wendy asked. "Is your love for him still coming to the boil, or have you put him on the back burner?"

Melissa did not know what to say. She had seen him with his wife on several occasions but had fortunately managed to avoid them both by heading off in the opposite direction or keeping herself locked inside the dressing-room or the caravan. Benjamín had been round to the van on several occasions, asking for her, but the girls had said she was out. Melissa could not bring herself to face the embarrassment. How could she say hello to his wife, knowing that she had been going out with him behind her back? When she thought of all the times he had brazenly taken her out, walked hand in hand, kissed her, and told her all his false dreams for their future relationship together, she felt so cheap and used that she could not bear to look at him. "I guess you could say that my feelings for him are hovering at the cold to freezing mark."

Wendy nodded her head, "Uh-huh, and you Sarah? What's happening with old Fernando?" She racked her brains to think of a trapeze related quip. "Er... is your romance in full swing, or are you about to swing for him?"

Sarah grinned. "Very droll, I must say! To be honest, He's so busy with the new tricks that we hardly see each other. He's a nice guy though, so, to answer your question, no, I'm not about to swing for him!" She surprised herself with her words. She realised that perhaps she did have some feelings for him. He was a nice guy and she could do a lot worse. Then she doubted herself. She wondered if her feelings could be blinkered by the thought of her future hopelessness. *Am I clinging on to him just to have a home?* She mentally shook herself. No...she did not think so.

"And so, we come to the lovely Lisa..." Wendy faltered, as all eyes turned to focus on the youngest member of the group. They felt as though they were seeing her for the first time. She looked broken, weak, and vulnerable. They realised that she had been quiet and almost none conversational since the party. They had all been so caught up in their own affairs that she had sort of slipped past them all.

"Er, how are you love?" Wendy's concerned tone forced Lisa into action.

"I'm fine! I don't want to talk about it!" She jumped up and almost ran out if the caravan.

Melissa stood up to bring her back, but Wendy stopped her.

"Let her go, Mel, she's not ready to tell us yet. But I bet that bastard has dumped her or something. I haven't seen him sniffing around since the party."

"That's true," Sarah replied. "Poor thing, I hope she'll be alright."

"She'll get over it. She's young. She's got a lot to learn and you only learn through your mistakes."

"Yeah, but the thing is, when does this bloody learning stop? Because I'm getting a bit sick of making mistakes, to be honest!" Melissa replied.

Wendy held her arm aloft and angled her glass towards the centre of the van. "I'll drink to that," she said as the other two drew nearer together and clinked glasses in unison.

In the early hours of the morning, while the three girls were in bed and half asleep, they heard the handle of the door jiggling up and down. Thinking it was Lisa, they waited for her to enter, but when they distinctly heard the clatter of metal on the step outside and a male voice whisper a harsh: "Shit!" it became apparent that they were mistaken.

Wendy jumped up from her bed and ran to the door.

"FUCK OFF AND LEAVE US ALONE!" She yelled into the darkness. The perpetrator set off running when he heard movement inside the van, but Wendy could make out his form as he ran into the darkness. She could not believe her eyes. For some reason, the man was dressed in a full clown costume! A vivid white satin suit complete with a net ruffle piped with red was around his neck. He was wearing a bright orange curly wig with a matching white hat and a yellow flower on a spring that flopped up and down as he ran. The only accessory missing from his weird attire was the huge clown shoes. This guy wore trainers for a swift getaway.

Wendy stood there, momentarily stunned. Why on earth was this guy dressed up like that in the early hours of the morning? Remembering that all the costumes were safely tucked away in the theatre, Wendy knew that this was an outsider. Someone who, it would appear, did not know the normal workings of a circus.

"Come back, you coward. Come back and fight like a man!"

The clown turned. In a split second, Wendy heard a pop and registered the flash of a firearm. Instinct made her dodge back inside the rusty old van when a bullet ricocheted off the metal door making a pinging noise that echoed around the site. Instantly lights came on inside all the adjoining vans, curtains twitched or were pulled back as everyone peered into the darkness. The man had gone but within a minute almost everyone was outside searching for the mysterious clown figure.

Flashing blue lights accompanied by weird sounding sirens soon filled the air as three police cars swarmed onto the site. The circus became alive with activity. Floodlights were rigged up to illuminate the entire area and police set about securing the scene. Several more police cars arrived, their occupants stood with notepads and pens taking witness statements.

The distinct contrast between the police force with uniforms and boots compared to the dressing-gowns and slippers of the circus cast was self-evident to Melissa who was severely shaken by the incident. Not only had she realised that Wendy could have been killed if she had not reacted so quickly, but she also realised that she had escaped death herself. The ricocheting bullet would have quite possibly killed her if it had not hit the silver-coloured strip that ran around the middle of the caravan like a seventies disco belt. The trailer may be a decrepit rust bucket, but it had saved their lives.

Her heart skipped a beat when she saw Benjamín coming sauntering towards the scene of the crime. He volunteered to translate for Wendy who was extremely grateful, even though she knew that Melissa had, once again, been put in a compromising situation.

The last vehicle to arrive was an ambulance whose occupants insisted on giving Wendy a check over. They wanted to take her to the hospital but she flatly refused, so they bundled her into the back of the ambulance. Benjamín stood by the back doors translating.

Lisa walked around the periphery of the scene and managed to slink inside the caravan hoping not to be questioned by the police. Not that she had witnessed anything anyway. She had been to speak to Mario, as she had done for the last two nights, but according to his mum, he was not there. Tonight, María had not even bothered to swing her bulk to the door, she had inched open a side window and bellowed his absence to the entire circus, making Lisa feel so embarrassed. She wished María really could make her shrivel up so that she could slither across the grass into the night.

Melissa soon followed Lisa inside. She had wanted an excuse to get away from the scene and as far away from Benjamín as possible. She had stood outside, keeping her distance and feeling like a spare part, a square peg in a round hole as her mother used to say. The longer she stayed in that environment, watching the man she thought she loved interacting with Wendy and the first-aiders the more hurt, used and upset she felt.

While he translated, Benjamín watched Melissa sneaking inside her van. He wanted to run over, grab her and try to explain, but he knew that now was not the right time. He also did not want to make a scene. It angered him that she was ignoring and avoiding him. He had tried on several occasions to speak to her and even gone to the caravan, but the girls had always told him she was out - even when he had seen her enter. All he wanted was the chance to explain.

When the police had taken statements and the ambulance had gone, curiosity waned and the artists returned to the comfort of their beds. The only lights that continued to burn were from the girls' caravan. In bed, but unable to sleep, they discussed the incident and wondered what was going on.

"Do you think it could be your husband?" Lisa questioned Wendy.

"I know for certain that the shooter wasn't my husband, but I do think he's behind it."

"Bloody hell, I feel like I'm taking part in a thriller movie. I'm a pawn in a game I have no control of and I don't bloody like it," Sarah's voice rose with every uttered clause, clearly highlighting her fear. "I mean, they haven't caught anyone, have they? How do we know they're not going to come back? Maybe even tonight!"

"They won't be back tonight. There's been too much activity for this evening. But, tomorrow, who knows?"

"You can't know that for sure!" Sarah snapped.

"Jesus!" Lisa muttered through clenched teeth. She remembered back to her idealistic ideas of circus life that she had divulged on the plane. She could not believe how wrong she could have been.

A brusque rap on the door startled them all. They froze, wrapped in fear, unable to move. Their eyes darted from one to another unsure what to do.

Wendy finally found her voice, "¿Sí?"

"It is I, Edwaldo," came the gruff voice. "Open the door."

Melissa clambered over Lisa and complied.

"Okay girls?" Forcing a smile, Edwaldo beckoned one of the circus security guards towards their door. "This is Carlos. He is going to be posted outside your caravan every night until we get to the bottom of all this, okay?" He heard the relieved sigh from within the van. "Now, try and get some sleep."

Carlos tipped his cap with a finger and smiled. "Hola!" When he received no reply from the stunned girls, he retreated and assumed his position outside the kitchen window.

Melissa closed the door again and let out a nervous giggle. "This is so ridiculous! Who would have thought that we'd end up in the middle of Brazil in such a mess?"

Wendy switched off the light. "I feel slightly safer knowing that Carlos is outside, but we have no idea how vigilant he will really be. Let's face it, would you take a bullet for some foreign girl you've never even spoken to?" The silence inside the caravan answered her question. "No, I didn't think so either!"

They settled down to a fitful sleep.

∽

By six o'clock that same morning, Sarah and Wendy had left the caravan and were on their way to the town centre. Neither one had hardly slept. The need to escape the confines of their claustrophobic home seemed to take priority and overrode everything else.

Carlos had tipped his cap again when they left and had maintained his stoic position by the kitchen window; legs astride and hands clasped behind his back as he scanned the area for intruders. He looked exhausted, which only made Wendy ponder how alert and on the ball he would be if the shooter put in another appearance.

Breaking into her thoughts, Sarah said: "I'm not sure we'll find anywhere open at this ungodly hour of the morning, but I needed to get out."

"There's bound to be a bakery or something open somewhere. Let's keep walking."

∽

Melissa and Lisa had heard the door close gently behind Wendy and Sarah. They lay there staring at the sun that shone through the thin curtains, bathing them in a warming yellow glow.

Melissa turned to Lisa. "I can't sleep, I'm going to make some coffee, do you want one?"

"Yes please," Lisa hitched herself up to a sitting position. "What a night! Do you think the shooter will come back, whoever he is?"

"Let's hope not, but if Wendy's husband is as bad as she says he is, then I think it's more than likely, yes."

Lisa hung her head and sighed.

Melissa assessed her friend and surmised that there was more to her demeanour than worrying about last night. "What's going on Lisa? What is it that you're not telling me?"

Lisa looked up with tears in her eyes and told her what had happened the night of the party. "The thing is that I haven't started my period. I'm ten days late, and I'm usually as regular as clockwork."

"You could be wrong. Don't jump to conclusions. You should take a test. I'll come with you to the pharmacy if you like."

"Will you?"

"Of course!" She passed Lisa the coffee. "Let's have something to eat, get washed and dressed, and then we'll go out and find a chemist's."

Their plans were thwarted when a ring boy knocked on the door asking for Melissa and Sarah.

"You come Sienna's trailer," he curtly addressed Melissa.

"Sarah isn't here," Melissa explained.

The boy frowned, not entirely sure what she was talking about.

Melissa returned the frown, "Sarah no aquí," she said in broken Spanish. The boy's puzzled expression angered her.

"You go Sienna's trailer," he repeated before spinning on his heels and getting as far away from the crime scene as possible.

"Oh for God's sake, what does the silly bitch want now?" Melissa said, addressing Lisa.

Lisa sipped her coffee, "I dread to think."

Forty-five minutes later, freshly showered, dressed, and fed, Melissa made her way over to Sienna's trailer. She knocked on the door and waited.

Edwaldo opened the door and beckoned her inside. "Come, come, Sienna is waiting."

Melissa walked inside, expecting to see the immaculate abode she had been privy to when they had first arrived, but the whole place was in disarray. Two older WAGs, who did not participate in the show, sat surrounded by mounds of material as they worked on two sewing machines. Sienna was at a third, barking orders across the table. She looked up when Melissa approached.

"Ah, yes, Melissa, come, I have new costumes for you and Sarah." While she fumbled under a mound of other show clothes, the bathroom door opened and out stepped Benjamín.

Melissa gasped, her hands flew to her mouth and she immediately looked away. Her entire body stiffened with nervous tension, she wanted to turn and flee, but she knew that she could not do so without making a scene and giving Sienna and her cronies something to gossip about.

"Melissa," Benjamín voiced as he walked towards her, "we have to talk." His tone was low, almost a mutter but sufficiently loud enough for the sewing trio to stop work and prick up their ears.

She ignored him, yet her body felt as though it were on fire. Their sexual tension coupled with their feelings of betrayal and hurt seemed to reach out and intertwine like tendrils of blue electricity fizzing in the air.

"I'll come and find you after the shows, okay?"

Not wanting to make a scene, Melissa kept her eyes cast downwards but acknowledged his statement with a curt nod.

He stood for a few seconds, willing her to look at him. He wanted to say more, but he was reluctant to give Sienna and her seamstresses something to revel in and gossip about later. "Okay then," he strode out of the trailer with a determined gait, taking Edwaldo with him.

Sienna held up Melissa's tiger-striped leotard from the magic act and graced her with a sly smile.

"Put it on," Sienna pushed the costume into her hands and stood with her hands on her hips watching with amusement.

Unsure as to why Sienna was so amused, Melissa stripped down to her underwear and stepped into the leotard. Once she had placed her second arm into the sleeve, Sienna approached her with an eagerness that bordered on exhilaration. She pushed Melissa towards the huge, mirrored doors at the end of the room. Melissa's mouth dropped open when she realised that Sienna had made alterations to the costume. These included a hood that fastened under her chin with two tiger shaped ears on the top of her head. As if that was not enough, Sienna presented her with a pair of flat pumps that had been covered in the same material as the leotards and made into a pair of knee-high boots. Sienna stood back to enjoy her handiwork, her eyes narrowing with her deviousness. She was more than certain that this would put an end to the daily wolf whistles that the girls had been receiving on too frequent a basis.

Melissa looked at the new, not so improved, version of herself. Her legs were no longer contoured, the muscles did not stand out as they did in high heeled shoes, and her hair was scraped back and hidden underneath a hood fit for a six-year-old's fancy dress party. She looked ridiculous. She was fuming. Her interaction with Benjamin was still festering inside her and she needed to release the anger which was bubbling up to the surface and reaching boiling point.

"But, Sienna, this looks like a child's costume. I thought the whole idea of this big, extravagant theatre show was to look elegant and sexy. Now, we're going to look like characters from a bloody children's party!"

Sienna wafted away her comments with a flick of her wrist. "No, no, no, this is much better. And the children will like the outfit. The show has to cater for children too. Now, get dressed. You can go. Tell Sarah to come later."

Melissa was livid. She pulled the costume off in a fit of rage and threw it onto the nearest chair. Dressing quickly, she walked out without saying goodbye and let the caravan door slam shut behind her.

Wendy and Sarah had returned by the time Melissa came stomping into the caravan.

"What the hell's the matter with you?" Wendy asked.

"Sarah, Sienna wants to see you in her trailer," Melissa began and poured out the entire story. While Sarah listened with growing anger and a shocked expression on her face, Wendy and Lisa tried to refrain from giggling as they imagined Sarah in her not so improved costume.

"I told you!" Wendy reminded them. "I said she was jealous of all your attention. She wants to be the 'número uno', and you two are threatening that."

Sarah stood for a moment deep in thought, then she pushed her feet into her clogs. "Okay then, let's get this over with." She pushed up her chin, drew her shoulders back, and walked out of the caravan. As she travelled the distance from her trailer to Sienna's, her mind was working overtime. Unlike Melissa, Sarah knew what to expect, and she was determined not to give Sienna the satisfaction that she craved. She tapped on the door and pulled it open. Poking her head inside with a huge smile plastered across her face, she said: "Sienna, I believe you wanted to see me?"

Sienna's face lit up with gleeful anticipation. She was more than ready for round two of her gratification and Sarah's humiliation.

"Yes, Sarah, come in. I suppose Melissa has told you that I've made some changes to the costume?" the question hung in the air like a bad smell.

"Er, actually no, she hasn't. She just said you wanted to see me."

Sienna's grin stretched even further across her face. "Oh, well then. Get undressed and I'll find your costume."

The process was repeated and Sienna pushed Sarah towards the mirrors so she could get a clear view of her expression of abhorrence.

Sarah, on the other hand, was well prepared. As Sienna flicked up the hood and fastened it under the chin, Sara's face broke into a broad smile. She turned to a surprised Sienna and clapped her hands, "Oh, wow! I just love it!" she bent her knees and swayed from side to side. She held up her hands to the sides of her face and made claw-like gestures and tiger growls into the mirror.

Sienna, standing to one side, was lost for words. Her smile slid from her face like an ice-cream from a cone on a hot summer's day. While Sarah continued doing tiger impressions and adopting different poses in front of the mirror, Sienna glanced at the two seamstresses. Their dumbfounded expressions as they looked back at her showed their confusion. They had been waiting for a similar reaction to Melissa's. The trio was sorely disappointed by Sarah's enthusiasm.

Sienna remembered the botched boots, picked them up, and shoved them towards Sarah. "Here, put these on..." she scrutinized Sarah's face for any sign of disappointment, but it was not forthcoming.

"Oh, fabulous! Matching boots too!" Sarah pulled her feet into the ugly, flat footwear and continued giving the performance of her life in front of the mirror.

The WAGs and an astounded Sienna looked on surprised and unsure how they should react to Sarah's enthusiasm.

As a final touch of brilliance, she turned and grabbed Sienna by the elbows. "Thank you, Sienna, I simply love it!"

Sienna was momentarily lost for words. Her frown and her inability to reply secretly pleased Sarah.

Minutes later, Sarah handed back the costume and almost skipped out of the trailer while Sienna and the seamstresses looked at each other again in abject bewilderment.

Back at the caravan, Sarah was a little disappointed to find that Melissa and Lisa had gone out. This meant that her only audience was Wendy. Sarah recounted her story about the costume and Sienna's face until Wendy doubled up on the bed, holding her sides from laughing so much.

"Oh, I wish I could have been there!" she said through bouts of laughter. "That must have been hilarious!"

෴

Lisa and Melissa stood inside a cubicle in the public toilets of a small cafeteria. Melissa had read the instructions with lowered tones, not wanting anyone else to realise what they were about to do. Lisa stood, deep in thought, tapping the end of a pregnancy test over and over in her hand.

Slightly irritated, Melissa whispered: "Are you going to do this or not? We can't stay in here together for much longer. People might start talking!"

"Oh, sorry, yeah!"

"Do you want me to wait outside, you know, while you do it?"

"Okay."

"Right," Melissa unlatched the door. "Do it, then wait two minutes and I'll come back in." She heard Lisa fumbling around and the trickle of urine as she tried to position the white stick in the correct position. Melissa glanced at her watch and timed the two minutes. When there was a deadly silence from the other side of the toilet door, she decided to wait a bit longer. When the second hand of her watch slowly completed two more revolutions, Melissa put her head as close to the door without touching it as she dared. "Are you alright in there? How's it going?" She heard the catch pull back and Lisa stood there, red-eyed and dejected. She thrust the stick forward. Melissa avoided touching it but stared down at the two tell-tale lines.

"Oh, Lisa, I'm so sorry."

Lisa let out a heart-wrenching wail.

"Don't cry, it'll be alright. We'll sort this out. Whatever you decide, I'll help you, okay?"

"Mario won't even talk to me," Lisa sobbed, releasing all the pent up tension that had been slowly building up since that fateful night.

Melissa's spine stiffened in anger that he could use a young girl in such a fashion and discard her like a piece of trash when he had got his way. "Maybe not, but he'll talk to me. Don't you worry."

As soon as they arrived back at the site, Melissa turned to Lisa.

"Okay, there's no time like the present. Let's head over to his van now."

Lisa grabbed her arm. "Are you sure?"

"Positive." She grasped Lisa's elbow and marched her over to Mario's home. Once again, he was not at home, so the girls veered over to his parent's trailer. They found the front door open and Mario sitting outside on one of three fold-up chairs, drinking beer with his friends. His eyes narrowed when he saw the two girls approaching. He made to stand up, but Melissa held up a hand, silently ordering him to stay seated. Keeping her hand in the same position she looked across at his two mates. "I think you two should go." Her steely glare caused both of them to jump up. They were well aware that something serious was about to happen.

"¿Estarás bien, Mario?" (will you be okay?) one of them uttered, not wanting to leave his friend to face one irate woman and a tearful sidekick.

Mario gave a nonchalant flick of his wrist, "yeah, no problem."

Melissa motioned for Lisa to sit down, but she remained standing.

"Lisa is pregnant with your baby. What're you going to do about it?" she said, getting straight to the root of the problem.

Mario squirmed uncomfortably in his seat and avoided eye contact with either of them. When he finally looked up, there was fury behind his eyes.

"Oh yeah? And who says it's mine?"

"Because, when you took advantage of her and had sex with her while she was drunk, she was a virgin. That's why I say it's yours."

Mario froze, he could not think straight. He bought some time by executing a contrived yawn, stretching his arms towards the sky as he assessed his situation with frantic urgency. He had no idea that he had been the first, but even so, he was too young to get lumbered with the responsibility of a child. Plus, his mother would probably kill him! He jumped up, putting himself on the same level advantage as Melissa. "That's not true. She's been with Miguel and a couple of others that I know about."

"No she hasn't you lying bastard," Melissa stepped closer to him, pure malice for him as a person and for his behaviour made her want to rip his eyes out. She shoved him hard in the chest. He fell backwards, his arms flailing, but he managed to steady himself.

"Hey!" he said marching towards her.

"Hey, nothing!" she shoved him again, taking out her anger over Benjamín's deceit, on Mario. "Now, what are you going to do about it?"

"Me?" he gave her a look of sheer bewilderment. "Why are you asking me? I told you, she's nothing to me. She's a little whore. I'm not the father!"

Melissa spun round to Lisa. "What's his mother's name again?"

"María," Lisa squeaked.

Melissa turned back and bellowed through the open door: "MARÍA!"

Lisa got slowly to her feet as the familiar lunging and squeaking of the protesting van supported the trajectory of Mario's mother.

María stopped in the doorway and took in the situation. She nodded her head with slow precision as she correctly assessed the situation before her.

Melissa made direct eye contact. "Lisa is pregnant," she mimed a bulging stomach with both hands. "And Mario is the father."

María's head turned slowly towards her son. She refrained from speaking as she looked him up and down. A contemptuous snarl forced her top lip to rise like a rabid dog about to attack. Her voice rose to a crescendo and a barrage of Spanish spat from her mouth.

Mario hung his head and almost cowered under her retort.

Despite the lack of language, it was more than obvious that María ordered him inside the van. He stood up, stomped with defiance to the door, and squashed past his mother to the relative safety of the van.

María turned to the girls. "Come back tonight, after the shows, we talk." She reached forwards, grabbed the door, and banged it shut.

The two girls looked at each other. Melissa boiling with inner rage and Lisa in floods of tears.

"Thank you," she said sobbing.

"Try not to worry. We'll get this sorted out," Mellissa patted her on the shoulder and steered her away.

That night, before the show, Sarah felt a cold sliver of doom run down her spine which made her visibly shiver.

Wendy noticed it. "What's up with you? You look like someone just walked over your grave."

"I don't know; I can't explain it. I have a really strong sensation like something is going to go wrong."

"Like what?"

"I don't know." She looked across at Wendy. "Forget it, I'm probably being silly."

"No," Wendy looked directly into Sarah's eyes. "I'm a big believer of sixth sense. But, it could be because of Lisa's news."

Sarah screwed up her nose and shook her head. "I don't think so. I honestly don't know what it is, but something just seems off."

"Then you be careful on the web tonight. I don't like you and Melissa doing that. It looks bloody dangerous to me. One slip and you'd come crashing to the ground like a sack of potatoes..." Once she had said it, she immediately regretted it. "Sorry, I don't mean to frighten you any more than you already are. Just be careful, okay?"

Sarah nodded.

"It could just be all the tension," Wendy continued, "you know, what with Melissa being upset about Benjamín; Lisa, Mario, and the baby; the shooting... I mean it's all going to build up and it's got to come out somewhere."

"Five minutes!" the stagehand announced over the tannoy with a seriousness that made the girls think they were about to attend a funeral, not perform in a show. They stood up and made their way to the backstage to put on their drums.

During the interval, Lisa ran to the toilets crying when Mario walked past her, made no eye contact but muttered: "whore" as he passed.

Melissa paced the dressing-room. On tenterhooks about her scheduled talk with Benjamín, she had continued to avoid him whenever possible. She had already decided that she was going to tell him their relationship was over. She needed to be with someone whom she could trust. She should have listened to her inner instinct from the beginning. She had always believed that he was hiding something, but she had hoped it would not be something so important as a wife and possibly even children.

Sarah remained quiet. She could not shrug off the niggling

feeling of ill-fated doom. Something was going to happen, but she had no idea what. Despite Wendy's warning about the web, that had been unnecessary. Sarah had seen her spying through the curtain during their act, but everything had been fine. The negative vibes in the dressing-room were overpowering her. She excused herself and went backstage.

Fernando stood preparing his hands with the powdered resin and tying the straps around his wrists. He looked up and smiled when he saw her approaching.

"Hi, how's it going?" he searched her eyes for clarity. She seemed so down. "What's the matter?"

Sarah sighed and tried to smile. "Oh, it's nothing!" she shook her head to verify how unimportant it was. "How are things with you?"

"Fine," his smile turned into a grin. "Excellent in fact. The new tricks have been going well. They're difficult, but I love performing them. By the way, my dad told me to tell you that you can start coming to the practices again." He flashed her a seductive smile. "He told me that he thinks you will make a good flyer. He wants to offer you a position in the group!"

Sarah's mouth opened in shock. "Really?"

"Yeah, he thinks you are ... now, how did he word it? ` True circus material´!"

"Wow! I'm honoured."

"Yeah, he said that, maybe, you were a circus artist in a past life." He grinned at Sarah's reaction.

The reference to past lives made her cringe. She felt like cosmic connotations were floating around, just beyond her grasp that made her shiver with fright.

"Five minutes to curtain, five minutes to curtain," came over the tannoy, and Sarah was relieved to excuse herself and prepare for the opening routine. "Be careful, Fernando," she said.

"I always am," he grinned.

. . .

Waiting in the wings to perform the tiger trick, Melissa looked across at Sarah and laughed. "Sorry, but I can't help it. You look so different with the tiger ears and clumpy boots."

"This is true," Sarah said looking down at her costume and lifting her hands to feel the little tiger ears on top of her head. Then she waggled a finger in Melissa's face, "but I still intend to get wolf whistles, just to piss Sienna off."

Melissa stopped laughing. "How do you intend to do that?"

"With Pizzazz, dear girl, with pizzazz!" She ran her hands down her body and smiled at Melissa with a wicked gleam in her eyes.

Melissa frowned.

Sarah registered Melissa's puzzled expression and decided to elucidate. "For example, when we walk on stage, we don't clomp on walking heel-toe-heel- toe, like a couple of miners in these god-awful boots. Oh no, we walk on the balls of our feet. That way the definition in our legs will still be there." She gave Melissa a short demonstration. "You see?"

Melissa nodded.

"We must dazzle the audience with our radiant smiles and move with a certainty that expresses that we are well aware of our sexual prowess." She gave another short demonstration. "Prowess, tigress... you get where I'm coming from?"

Melissa nodded and smiled. Her eyes sparkled as she registered the truth in Sarah's words.

"And that way," Sarah continued, "we will still get more attention from the audience than silly Princess Sienna," she said, finishing with a cunning grin.

The music started and on they walked, exuding sexuality with every precise step.

Sarah cast Melissa a victorious glance when the whistling began.

Once inside the trick, they shuffled down into their hidden position and held hands while the mighty tiger plodded with disdain above their heads. Unexpectedly, it let out a deep roar and both girls jumped. Then they felt a hot, steaming liquid pour through the cracks and cover their upper bodies and faces.

"For fuck's sake. It's tiger piss!" Sarah spat to keep the acrid taste out of her mouth.

Despite their predicament, Melissa could not hold back her giggles. "Perhaps this is what you were worrying about before the show! This is Karma. It looks like Sienna's got the last laugh after all."

The cage was wheeled into the wings with the girls still hidden inside it. Sienna entered the stage, oblivious to what had happened to the girls inside the cage but annoyed that her childlike costumes had not had the desired effect she was looking for.

Lisa stood at the side of the stage, deep in thought, waiting to perform the water illusion. She did not sense anyone was behind her until Miguel touched her lightly on the shoulder.

"Hi," he said. "Are you alright?"

His genuine concern caught her unawares and her eyes filled with tears. "Not really."

"I've heard what's happened," he said.

"I hate him!" Lisa heard herself saying. "I swear to you Miguel, it's Mario's baby. I haven't slept with anyone else. And I only slept with him once."

He patted her arm. "You don't have to tell me anything. I don't believe a word that guy says anyway, but I do believe you."

"Thank you."

"Look, I'd like to invite you out for a meal this evening," he held up a hand as Lisa was about to interrupt. "You need to eat well for the baby. You don't need to talk about anything that you are uncomfortable with. I'm just offering you the hand of friendship, okay?"

Lisa put both hands over her face and roughly swiped away the tears. "Okay, thank you." Wendy's words of wisdom echoed through her brain as she recalled how Wendy had tried to steer her away from Mario and push her towards Miguel.

∼

After the show, Melissa and Lisa walked across the site to Mario's trailer. Lisa was going under duress. She knew that it needed to be done, but she was dreading even the thought of the meeting. Melissa felt the same, but she wore a contemptuously arrogant facial expression, determined to get some sort of compensation from that arsehole of a so-called boyfriend.

Mario opened the door when they knocked. Giving them both a surly sneer of contempt, he refrained from acknowledging them further and merely stood back to let them both inside. His mother sat on a wide armchair, her bulk made the girls wonder how she had even managed to squash herself into the seat in the first place. She motioned for them to sit down with a flick of her finger. They sat together on the sofa, feeling dwarfed by the huge woman and uncomfortable in unfamiliar surroundings.

"So, you say my son is the father of this ...baby," getting straight to the point, she flicked a hand in Lisa's direction.

"Yes," Melissa stated with conviction, while Lisa sat there astounded at how good María's English was. She realised that María must have revelled in Lisa's discomfort every time she had tried to converse in the past.

"But...how do you know?" Maria gave a short laugh, expressing that even the assumption of her son being the father was bordering on the ridiculous. "What proof do you have?"

"Well, none at the moment," Melissa replied, "but..."

"Then, why are you wasting my time? What do you expect me to do? My son is not going to spend the next twenty years paying for a child that may or may not even be his!"

"There are paternity tests," Melissa's strength grew as she realised that her reply had abruptly stopped María's laughter. "But in the meantime. We are going to need some sort of financial support. As we say in England, 'it takes two to tango'," she saw Maria's confusion. "In other words, they both caused the problem, so they'll both have to deal with it."

"What does she want to have the baby for anyway? She's young, she could get rid of it."

"You do know that abortion is a crime in this country, don't you?" Melissa counter attacked. "She could go to jail for three years if she even attempted to have an abortion."

Maria snorted. "There are ways..."

"Yes, I agree, that's true, María," Melissa replied. "Lisa could have your son arrested for rape and then she would be legally allowed to have an abortion. Would you like us to do that?"

María began chuntering under her breath, the volume gradually rose until she was shouting at the top of her voice at her recalcitrant son. He stood with his head down taking all that she threw at him and not replying.

Then she turned on the girls. "How do we know she's even pregnant? This could be extortion!"

Lisa fiddled around in her purse and held out the white stick with the two lines.

María began shouting again. This progressed to throwing a cushion at her son's head. It bounced off, making him step back and it landed with a dull thud on the caravan floor, which for some reason Melissa found highly amusing.

When María stopped shouting, Melissa knew that she had won. Mario's mother looked exhausted and beaten.

"Okay, give me a few days," María said, her sullen tones expressed her annoyance. "And we'll come to some sort of agreement in regards to money."

"Very well," Melissa stood up and Lisa followed.

They brushed past Mario and stepped outside. The cool air felt good on both their faces as they headed back towards their caravan. Melissa was surprised that María had finally acquiesced after seeing the pregnancy test. At the end of the day, a white stick with two lines on it did not necessarily make Mario the father. She guessed that María knew her son only too well and she could not deny that Lisa had been hanging around their trailer night after night inquiring after her son.

Lisa was so relieved. "Thank you. Melissa. Thank you so much!"

"Any time, Lisa. Any time," she said, surprised by her victory and surprised by her behaviour. She realised that circus life was beginning to toughen her up but she thought that, under the circumstances, that had to be a good thing.

Twenty minutes later the two girls were in their caravan seeking moral support as they waited for Benjamín and Miguel. This time it was Melissa`s turn to be in the most uncomfortable social position.

Benjamín arrived first but when he tried to steer Melissa away, she refused. "Let's wait for Miguel to arrive first and then I'll talk to you."

"Miguel?" Benjamín looked confused, "don't you mean…"

"Shh!" Melissa was not about to divulge Lisa's story or make her feel more uncomfortable than she already was. "Yes, Miguel!" she snapped. Her facial expression made him refrain from further questioning.

Just then, the juggler came walking around the corner. Lisa was surprised to see him all dressed up. He acknowledged Melissa and Benjamín before addressing Lisa. "Hi. Are you ready to go?"

She gave a demure nod, and they sidled away, walking side by side, a distance of half a metre between them.

Benjamín stared down at Melissa. "What's going on there?"

"It's a long story." She snapped.

Her curt response shocked him. "Thank you for agreeing to speak to me," he mumbled. "Perhaps now, we can sort this mess out. Can I interest you in some dinner?"

Melissa realised that she was starving. She had hardly eaten all day, worrying about this meeting and the arranged confrontation with María. She nodded her head. "Yes."

"Okay, let's go."

They found a quaint looking Italian Bistro. The waiter took their order, poured the wine, and left them in peace. Benjamín was all smiles as she sat opposite him. He had no idea her stomach felt like a ship navigating on a stormy sea. Her hands were clenched into fists under the table, her nails dug into the palms of her hands, the pain helped to keep her focused. Her mouth was dry, despite an earlier swig of the red wine. She had decided to hear him out and then finish the relationship, but she was not prepared for the story that Benjamín was about to tell her.

"First of all, I want to apologise for not introducing you to Mariela. I didn't get the chance on the first evening of the party..." He paused waiting for her reply, which was not forthcoming. "Er, and of course after that night, you seem to have done your best to avoid me."

Melissa took another good gulp of wine. She stared at giving her head an incredulous shake of disbelief. "Are you really surprised!" It was a statement rather than a question. She was not expecting a reply.

"Well, quite frankly, yes, I am."

Melissa was dumbfounded by his overt disregard for her feelings. "So, you think it's perfectly alright to start a relationship with me but omit to inform me that you are already married?" She shook her head a second time in bewilderment, but she was even more perplexed when his mouth split into a huge grin and he began to chuckle.

"What's so amusing?" she scowled, her whole body poised to flee. She contemplated jumping up and leaving him sitting there, cackling like some demented mental patient.

"Well, the thing is, Melissa, I'm laughing because Mariela isn't my wife!"

"Yeah, right," Melissa's condescending tone was unmistakable.

"Melissa, I swear to you. She's my sister!"

Melissa's mouth fell open, and she realised that she was the fool, not Benjamín.

"She came to watch the opening night at the theatre and to meet you. But you've been avoiding both of us like the plague!"

Melissa felt so stupid. Her mind flashed back to the party. She had mistaken their gestures of intimacy and familiarity as husband and wife, not brother and sister. "Oh, I'm so sorry!" she mumbled. "I've always thought that you were hiding something from me and I believed I'd uncovered it. I felt so stupid and so used." All her pent up tension evaporated, and she broke out laughing at her own stupidity.

"Don't you know how much I love you?" His words stopped her laughter in a millisecond.

"No, I didn't ..."

"I wanted her to meet you before I asked you to marry me."

"Er...what?" Her mind refused to register what she was hearing.

"Will you marry me, Melissa?"

Time stopped as Melissa digested his words, she had wasted the last two weeks fretting when she could have been in seventh heaven. "Yes," the word slipped out of its own accord, she heard it, yet she felt as though a higher being had spoken for her.

Benjamin's face broke into a wide grin. He slipped off his chair and landed on one knee. Reaching inside his jacket he extracted a blue, velvet box which, when opened, revealed an elegant, old diamond ring. He removed the piece of jewellery and slipped it onto her third finger. It fit perfectly. "Mariela brought this ring for me. It used to be our mother's."

Melissa's eyes filled with tears and she held out her arms like a child begging to be kissed.

~

Miguel held out a chair for Lisa to sit down. This simple gesture filled her eyes with tears. He sat opposite her and immediately passed her a serviette.

"Don't cry, everything will be okay, trust me." He signalled for the waiter and ordered in Portuguese for them both.

Lisa wiped her eyes and refrained from blowing her nose although she was desperate to do so.

"We'll have a nice meal and a chat, okay?" Miguel patted her hand.

She nodded in silent consent.

Miguel could not understand his own feelings. Here was a girl, apparently pregnant with another guy's baby and yet all he wanted to do was to hold her in his arms and keep her safe forever.

∼

By chance, the two couples arrived back at the circus entrance at the same time. The girls smiled at each other, both somehow intuitive in their reading of the other's situation.

Melissa smiled across at Lisa, "Everything good?" She was pleased to see Lisa's carefree smile appear on her face.

"Great, thanks, and you?"

Melissa held up her hand and showed off the diamond that sparkled with a myriad of colours in the moonlight.

Lisa gasped. "Oh, my God! Congratulations!" she hugged her friend.

Miguel shook Benjamín's hand and then they hugged, tapping each other on the shoulder blades. The typical 'all-male' hug that, in one embrace, encapsulates their happiness for their friend while outwardly portraying their status as straight men.

Melissa turned to Lisa. "Thanks, and you?"

"Miguel and I are a couple now."

"Then congratulations to you too!"

The two girls linked arms with their partners and set off walking towards the girls' caravan. Halfway across the site, there was an angry bellow, and Mario came rushing from the shadows, barging into Miguel and knocking him flat on the ground. The attack was so quick that Miguel was winded and Benjamín had yet to register what had happened. Mario straddled Miguel and began to pummel his face with angry fists, left and right left and right over and over again. Lisa jumped onto Mario's back. "Get off him, get off!"

Benjamín jumped in and dragged Mario off the bleeding Miguel.

"What the fuck are you doing?" he said, holding Mario by the scruff of his neck.

Mario ignored his captor and glared at Miguel. "Keep your filthy mitts off my girl," he snarled.

Miguel spat blood from his split lip, but before he had the chance to speak, Lisa screamed. She charged forward and punched Mario in the face. An action that released all her previously pent up emotions and she felt strangely jubilant. His lip burst and a spray of blood exploded into the night.

"I'm not your girl, I never have been and I never will be. You are a cold, arrogant child who has a lot of growing up to do. Even your own mother said you are no good."

She saw his face contort at her words and knew she had broken through his hard, macho façade. The comment about his mother had definitely hit home.

"I'm not paying you good money for a bloody kid and not getting any benefit out of it. You belong to me!"

"I don't want your money. I'm with Miguel now. I want you to leave me ALONE!"

Mario's eyes narrowed. "Maybe, but you are forgetting one important thing. The baby in your belly is mine, so you'll never truly be rid of me."

Their eyes locked. Neither one was willing to break away.

"Who says I'm going to keep it?"

The silence that enveloped stretched into eternity as Lisa's words hung in the silence. She turned, took Miguel's arm and they walked away.

While Mario sagged defeated, Benjamín loosened his grip on Mario's collar and pushed him away.

The foursome walked away from the tormented teen who had been thwarted by a girl. He watched her walk into the night, the darkness swallowing her up, and he knew that he had lost her forever.

THE CIRCUS AFFAIR

∽

The following morning, the girls were up early. After the activities from the night before: Melissa's engagement, Lisa's new love, and the horrible showdown with Mario they had hardly slept. They were sitting eating breakfast, two girls on each bed when there was a knock on the door.

Melissa opened it and was surprised to see Edwaldo standing there with a tall, good looking blond-haired man. She wondered if she and Lisa were in trouble. Remembering the fight, the previous night, she guessed that they were in for a considerable telling off, a reprimand, or maybe even a fine of some sort.

"Yes...?"

"May we come in," Edwaldo asked, his tone gave away no hint as to his visit or the identification of the stranger.

"Er..." Melissa glance back inside the caravan to see the others hastily pulling sheets over unmade beds, depositing their breakfast bowls in the kitchen sink, and squashing together at the far side of the van. "Yes, come in."

The caravan creaked at the excess weight and tilted on its axel as the two men bent their heads forward to enter the confined space. They sat close together on the little bed and looked at the four wide-eyed girls huddled together on the bed opposite.

"Girls, this is Detective Inspector Adam Green, he needs to talk to you all."

The stranger reached into his jacket pocket, flicked open a small leather holder, and gave them a quick flash of a badge.

"Are we in trouble?" Lisa nibbled on a fingernail and waited for an answer.

Edwaldo turned to the detective. "Adam, I think you will be able to explain this better."

Adam sat up straighter and look at the girls with an earnest expression on his face. "Okay, girls, what I'm about to tell you all concerns Wendy more than the rest of you, but it is imperative that you all listen and take heed of what I'm about to tell you."

Wendy noticed that he made direct contact with her when he spoke her name. He already knew who she was and that unnerved her.

"Wendy, the shooter from the other night was apprehended by the Brazilian police yesterday afternoon. He was trying to board a flight back to England. Under interrogation, we have discovered that he had been hired by your husband to kill you."

The three other girls gasped, but Wendy did not react. She had already guessed as much. Now that she had confirmation she just felt numb. In contrast, the other three were antsy, looking at each other in shock and jabbering like farmhouse hens in a chicken coup.

"Okay girls," Adam's authoritative voice immediately silenced the trio. "Calm down, please." Once again, he made direct eye contact with Wendy. "We have also discovered that your husband needs you dead to claim on the life insurance policy he took out on you three years ago. According to our source, your husband has made some dodgy drug deals recently that have lost him a lot of money, and he needs to find some quickly. I suppose bumping you off was the fastest option. He is said to be currently on the run, trying to avoid the Cartel Drug Lord Giovanni Rossi to whom he owes thousands and thousands of pounds."

Like a marionette, Melissa's mouth dropped open and remained there as if the puppeteer had relinquished the strings. "This is unbelievable. It's like something out of a film script." The girls nodded in agreement.

"We have no idea if he has ordered a further hitman to take over where the last one failed. Or if he plans to finish the job himself. Therefore, I have been sent to protect you until further notice," Adam explained. Then he turned his attention to the remaining girls. "I would suggest the rest of you find other accommodation for the time being. That way, you will hopefully be out of harm's way."

"Oh my god, I can't believe this!" Sarah voiced. "All those nights we heard someone moving about in the forest. We could have been shot at any time."

"Finally! I'll get the caravan all to myself. My cunning plan has worked." Wendy joked, but her attempt at sarcasm was lost on the terrified girls.

Edwaldo interrupted their train of thought. "Do you all have somewhere you could stay, or do you need my help?"

"We should be alright," Melissa replied.

Wendy thought about making another attempt at humour but decided against it. The situation was hardly a laughing matter, and the sooner the girls were in a safer place she would feel much more relaxed. She would not want any of them to get caught up in the crossfire.

Adam stood up. "Right then, I would suggest you do that as soon as possible girls because I intend sleeping in the caravan tonight."

The girls looked at him in awe. His head brushed the top of the caravan roof, his broad shoulders seem to block out the light behind him as he stood with his hands on his hips. His jacket gaped open to reveal the handle of his gun which peeked slyly from a snug, shoulder-holster. His mere presence seemed to cram the caravan to capacity and filled Wendy with a deep sense of calm. She could not explain it, but she felt that she would be safe with this guy around.

By the end of the afternoon, the girls had packed and moved out. Their dilemma had spread around the circus, like a deadly virus and before the hour was out, everyone had been infected with the news.

The girls hated the fact that basically, the entire circus had adopted positions outside their vans to watch the to-ing and fro-ing of the three girls but not one of them had offered to help.

Nobody was particularly surprised to see that Melissa would be staying with Benjamín. They had all heard about the engagement, so it seemed only natural under the circumstances. Lisa, on the other hand, was cause for gossip and speculation. They had all assumed she'd move in with Mario despite their turbulent relationship. Lisa had other plans. She had shyly asked Miguel, who had welcomed her with open arms. Fernando had heard the news before Sarah had even had a chance to talk to him. He came knocking on the door, checking if she was alright and insisting that she move in with him.

That evening, as the four girls sat in their dressing-room preparing for the show, Wendy giggled. "It seems so funny having a six-foot-two bodyguard standing outside our door. I feel like we're famous or something."

Sarah's eyes twinkled and she gave Wendy a playful nudge with her elbow. "Just think, tonight he'll be stood over your bed, like a blonde guardian angel."

"Or maybe even in it," Melissa joined in, "I mean, correct me if I'm wrong, but I'm pretty sure I heard him say that he needed to stay close to you."

"Not that bloody close!" Wendy laughed.

"Ooh! Wendy, your luck might be in tonight," Sarah elbowed her again.

All four of them turned to admire the physique of this tall stranger, who had come out of nowhere to unexpectedly save the day.

They ploughed through the show. They were already bored with it and felt as though they were going through the motions; churning out the same merchandise night after night, rather like an employee in a factory. Before they knew it, the first half was over. They were pottering about the dressing-room killing time when Adam poked his head in the door and excused himself.

"I'll be back in five minutes, nature calls! Keep vigilant girls."

The girls enjoyed the view as he sauntered away.

"Cast your eyes away, girls. He's mine!" Wendy joked.

By the time the orchestra struck up and played the opening music for the beginning of the second half, Adam was back at his post. The girls were still in the dressing-room changing for the magic act when the music for the flying trapeze came to a grinding halt. They heard an audible gasp from the audience, followed by a tense feeling of total stillness and shock that was deeply unnerving.

Artists began running towards the stage and the girls stood up to do the same.

Adam jumped into action and blocked their exit with his huge muscular arms. "Stay here," he ordered.

"What's going on?" Sarah said pushing to get past Adam's huge biceps that were holding all four of them back.

"Let us out," Melissa complained. "I want to see what's going on!"

"No," Adam replied, with an abruptness that shocked them all. "This could be a diversion to get everyone focused on something else so that the killer can come in here and shoot Wendy. This is a tactic that experienced killers use."

"But, surely, if we're on the stage with everyone else, we'd be safer than here on our own," Sarah argued.

Adam looked vexed and momentarily lost for words.

"Not if he's a sniper," Melissa replied.

In the silence that followed as the girls digested Melissa's comment, the brassy, insistent, tinny beep of an ambulance siren approaching grew louder and louder.

Sarah clasped a hand over her mouth. "Oh no! It's Fernando, he's had an accident!"

Lisa looked perplexed, "How do you know?"

"I just do." She pushed past Adam, ducking under his arm and ran towards the stage.

Melissa walked towards, their bodyguard. "Let me go. I need to check that she's okay. She shouldn't be on her own at a time like this."

Adam dropped his arms and let her pass. "Lisa, if you want to go, you can. I'll stay here with Wendy."

Lisa visibly shivered in her seat. "Thanks, but no thanks. I've got enough imagined pictures in my head, I don't think I could stomach the real thing."

Adam sighed, nodded and took his position at the door again.

Sarah reached the stage. Fernando's crumpled body lay on top of the fallen safety-net; blood poured from his mouth. She saw a nasty cut in his side, where one of the supporting wires had snapped and sliced into him like a hot knife in butter, causing blood to flow over the net. It puddled in each perfectly squared section, like mini jelly moulds still not set before spreading onto the wooden stage floor, a thick, glutinous liquid from which Sarah could not look away.

"Fernando," she ran to his side, just as the ambulance crew reached the stage. Someone pulled her away so the paramedics could get to work. She turned to find herself in Melissa's arms. "Is he going to be alright?"

Melissa glanced at his body. It looked deformed, as though he was a disregarded doll thrown to the floor by a recalcitrant child. The top half of his body seemed to be facing the wrong way around.

Melissa looked at her friend with such pity, Sarah dreaded hearing her words.

"If he survives this, I doubt he'll be flying anymore."

Sarah burst into tears and watched helplessly as he was stretchered out of the theatre.

Like all true showbusiness performers, Benjamín picked up the microphone and told the stunned audience that the show would go on. Gradually, the stage cleared, and the orchestra took their places in the pit.

Sarah viewed the ordeal as though she was outside of her own body, watching the proceedings from a higher level of existence. She saw some audience members get up and leave, obviously appalled that after such a major accident the other artists would continue the show like nothing had happened. Others remained, callously thinking about the cost of the tickets and getting their value for money.

The girls walked back to the dressing-room to a stunned duo who gently grilled them for information. Sarah sat in silence, hardly functioning as Melissa told them what she could. The girls were also shocked to discover that the rest of the show would go on as planned.

They heard Benjamín announcing the next act and realised that they needed to finish getting ready for the magic act. This time,

Adam let them pass and they performed the illusions with a numbness they could not seem to shake off.

At the end of the show, Benjamín announced to the audience, that the injured flyer had been taken to hospital and that he would be fine. The girls looked at each other and shook their heads. After Melissa's graphic description, they doubted that what Benjamín was saying would be true. Fernando was hardly likely to be back flying within the next few days. However, it made perfect sense that Benjamín's words would make the audience feel less ill at ease. They could go home and regale their family and friends with a story that had a happy ending.

Back in the dressing-room, Lisa continued bombarding Melissa and Sarah with questions. Asking in what position they had found him, how much blood there had been, and what was their impression of his possible injuries and recovery. In the end, Melissa snapped.

"Lisa, if you're so interested, why didn't you come out and see for yourself?"

Lisa shivered with revulsion, "I couldn't bring myself to see it for real. Look!" she pointed to her arm, "I've got goose-bumps just thinking about it."

That night, back at the site, the entire circus was subdued and quiet. Contrary to normality, the usually noisy atmosphere felt more like a funeral wake. The habitual music blaring from certain caravans, the shouted arguments of disgruntled couples, and the singing of others were ominously absent as they waited expectantly for more news.

"I think I should stay in the caravan with you, this evening, Wendy," Sarah said. "I don't feel it's right to go back to his trailer, especially as he isn't going to be there."

Adam shook his head. "No way! I still say that all of this could be a ploy to throw people off. Look how everyone is staying in the trailers rather than milling around the site like they normally do. No,

Sarah, I must insist that for your safety you spend the night in Fernando's van or bunk up with one of the other girls."

Sarah acquiesced but she did not feel comfortable doing so. She did not want to be alone in an unfamiliar caravan. As she walked back across the site to Fernando's trailer, a niggling sensation in the pit of her stomach gave her the feeling that she should sleep where she had always slept. Was that because she was afraid for Wendy or did it stem from something else? A brief thought about going around to Melissa and Benjamín's caravan and pleading loneliness and insecurity crossed her mind. But deep down, she knew she could not do that. She did not want to barge in on them when it was only their second night together as an engaged couple. She also did not feel as close a bond to Lisa as she did to Melissa. And Miguel, well, he felt almost like a stranger to her.

Wendy changed into her nightwear in the tiny bathroom, she would have normally done that in the caravan, but Adam was in there watching her every move. When she stepped out of the bathroom she saw his eyes appraise her and a satisfied smile widened across his face. He perused her body from the top of her uncombed hair down to her bare feet. The air felt full of static energy as though the slightest movement would send him running towards her. Feeling uncomfortable, Wendy said good night and got into bed. She spied the curtains at the ends of the bed and pulled them closed for the first time ever since moving in. She was grateful for the privacy. She could not seem to shake his lewd facial expression from her mind and it unnerved her. For the first time, her opinion of him changed. She had placed him on a pedestal as her knight in shining armour, her protector and saviour, but now, with one inappropriate gesture, he had come crashing down, falling on top of a pile of men who had all disappointed and hurt her in the past.

Sarah lay in the dark, her hands behind her head staring at the ceiling. She found it impossible to sleep. To her surprise, being alone in Fernand's trailer felt quite natural, but her mind refused to let her rest. She was worried about him, of course, but his family had said that they only wanted his immediate family to go to the hospital at the moment. The latest news from Edwaldo was that he had come out of surgery and he was stable, but that was not the reason for her inquietude. She felt that she was missing something that evaded her consciousness. A tiny clue just beyond her reach. Common sense told her to replay the events of the day and analyse them. Perhaps then, she might be able to get to the bottom of her sleeplessness. She thought about Adam's arrival. His appearance out of the blue had felt like a Godsend, but now she had her doubts. What did any of them actually know about him? He had flashed a badge that none of them had examined or even questioned. Sarah though back over the conversation. When the girls had agreed to move out, she remembered his words:

"I would suggest you do that as soon as possible because I intend to sleep in the caravan tonight."

She now found that statement odd. Why would a working Police Detective sleep in the same place as the possible victim? Surely it was his responsibility to stay awake and keep guard.

She reflected on his short disappearance during the interval and then his sudden presence after Fernando's accident. Had he tampered with the rigging? Had he caused the fall? His comment about snipers causing diversions also rang alarm bells in her head. Was he the sniper and playing some sort of mind game? Had he wanted everyone to go to the stage except Wendy so that he could kill her in the dressing-room and disappear while everyone else was focused on the accident?

Abruptly, her train of thought dissipated, and she began to doubt her own reasoning. If what she had been thinking was true, then what had thwarted his plan? Why hadn't he killed her and left while everyone else was indisposed? For a while, she reprimanded herself for her overactive imagination. Wendy was probably fine. Yet her mind refused to rest. She ruminated on the same questions over and over again. Stumped, and angry with herself for doubting a guy who had travelled from the other side of the world to protect her friend, she struggled to look at the situation objectively.

Sarah started again; assessing the events of the day. At the end of the show, when Lisa had been asking all the gory questions what was it she had said?

"I couldn't bring myself to see it for real."

Sarah jumped up. That was the reason. He had not been able to kill Wendy because Lisa had refused to leave the dressing-room. Perhaps he had been given orders not to kill the other girls.

Another thought flashed through her mind. When Sarah had suggested staying with them in the caravan, he had been against it. His comment raced through her brain and suddenly everything clicked.

"Look how everyone is staying in the trailers rather than milling around the site like they normally do."

How would he know what the circus folk normally did if he hadn't been surveying the scene for some time?

Sure of her deductions she scrambled out of bed. Wendy was in danger, but how could she, Sarah, possibly save her? She pulled on her clothes, left the caravan, and headed over to Lisa and Miguel's. Without explaining, she told them to get dressed and go over to Benjamín's trailer as quickly as possible. Then, she ran with urgency towards their trailer.

After being invited in by a drowsy Benjamín dressed in a long, maroon dressing-gown, Melissa emerged from the bedroom as Miguel and Lisa knocked on the door. Sarah recounted her thoughts and tried to convince them all that Wendy was in danger.

Melissa became agitated, she wholeheartedly agreed with Sarah. Lisa took a little longer, but pretty soon she was also worried about Wendy's safety. Benjamín and Miguel, on the other hand, took a little more convincing.

"But, if what you're saying is true," Benjamín began, "he must have convinced Edwaldo and he's no push-over as you both well know." He omitted to tell them that he had been in Edwaldo's trailer when Adam had knocked that morning. He had not paid particular attention to the flashed official badge either. Neither of them had. They had believed him without question.

Miguel finished ruminating on the situation and nodded his assent, he pointed in Sarah's direction. "What Sarah is saying all makes sense. What would a high ranking, British police official be doing in the middle of a circus in Brazil? Wouldn't the case be passed on to the Brazilian police force to handle?"

No one replied. No one knew the intricacies and legalities of such a case.

Sarah watched them, seeing their minds ticking over while they processed the extra information. Trying to urge them along she said: "Would he even have jurisdiction over here? Doesn't it make more sense that Adam is hiding in plain sight? I believe he's the assassin sent by Wendy's husband to replace the other one who botched the job."

"Maybe he's the original assassin," Melissa replied. "That would make sense of how he knows the habits of the circus folk. I don't believe the Brazilian police caught anyone for the first crime. I think it's him."

Benjamín finally nodded his head. "I think you're right, Melissa. Wendy is in danger, but how are we going to get her out of there without alerting Adam? I think we should go and tell Edwaldo." He grabbed Melissa's arm and they headed to the bedroom to throw on some clothes. Five minutes later, the motley crew set off for the biggest trailer on the site.

Edwaldo opened the door with a yawn. A look of total surprise crossed his face when he saw the group standing on his doorstep. "Hi, what's up?"

A disgruntled Sienna shuffled into view behind him. Devoid of make-up and with tousled hair she looked more like a long-haired Afghan hound called Princess than her usual buffered polished appearance they were all used to seeing.

Benjamín stepped passed Edwaldo. "Let us come in."

A few minutes later, Edwaldo was convinced that they were onto something, while Sienna remained obtuse and obstinate.

"Okay, first things first. We need to call the police and explain the situation. Sienna, get me my phone."

Despite the need for urgency, Sarah and Melissa glanced at each other with knowing hints of smiles. It felt good to know that, at least in her caravan, Sienna was the underdog.

"Now, we'll need to create a diversion..." Edwaldo turned to Benjamín, "Any ideas?"

"I thought about a fire. That would get everyone out and running around. That should give us enough time to get Wendy away from Adam's grasp – if we're not too late already." Benjamín replied. His words instilled dread in their hearts and Lisa began to cry.

Edwaldo continued. "Okay, Benjamín and the girls, go to the belly-box at the back of my caravan, get some of the fire-wood I keep there for the wood-burner, and pile it up at the edge of the site. Make sure it's far enough away from the other caravans, but strategically placed so that if Adam and Wendy see the flames, they'll think it's one of the vans. If anyone else hears you moving about and asks what's going on, tell them and get them to help. Miguel, you are the least likely to be associated with Wendy, so you are the one who will try and get her away from Adam. If he should see you hanging around, he wouldn't suspect you to know anything. We'll all run around knocking on the doors so that all the circus is out and running. That way, it should be easier for Miguel to slip away with Wendy. If only there was a way to warn her without Adam knowing."

"There is!" Sarah grinned. "Her mobile phone."

"Yes, but Adam will hear it."

"Not necessarily. We always put our phones on vibrate during the night. He might not hear it. And even if he does she can say she's texting me. That might delay him doing anything just yet."

"Good thinking, Sarah," Edwaldo smiled. "Okay, you stay here and try and contact her. I'll phone the police and the rest of you start getting the wood together."

~

Back in her caravan, Wendy could not sleep. She was also having niggling doubts. Why would Adam be lying in the caravan and not pacing the vicinity? Even the circus guards had been more vigilant than he seemed to be. Something was off with the entire situation. She heard her phone vibrate on the tiny ledge by her side and picked it up.

Adam's weight shifted on the bed. "What's that?"

Wendy glanced at the caller I.D. "It's a message on my phone." She read it and froze.

`Wendy you are in danger. Adam is the assassin!´
She heard him sit up.

"What does she want?" he asked.

`We are coming to help you,´ the phone buzzed again.

"Er...she said she can't sleep. She's upset about Fernando."

"Tell her to let you sleep. Tell her you're tired."

`We'll cause a diversion. Be ready. Go with Miguel.´

"well, er... the thing is, I'm not tired either. It's weird, but Sarah and I have had to share the same bed since the beginning of the contract and er... I can't seem to sleep without her." She stared at the closed curtains and regretted closing them earlier. Now, rather than maintain her privacy, she wanted to be watching his every move.

`Take care. We all love you and we'll get through this together xx´

She read the last message and wanted to cry. Then her helplessness morphed into a hidden strength. A sense of self-preservation and adrenalin ran havoc through her veins. On impulse, she deleted the messages, hid her phone under her pillow, and then grabbed the curtains and flicked them back with a flourish. Adam was out of bed, sitting with his feet on the floor, staring at her.

"Shit!" he muttered. "You made me jump."

Wendy's hair stood on end. The way he had muttered the expletive only convinced her that he was the same guy who had been trying to get into her caravan in the other town. Sarah was right. She was in the van with her assassin! She wondered why she was still alive. Why hadn't he killed her already?

"I need the toilet now!" she stood up, faking a smile. "Honestly! What a night! All I want to do is sleep and I can't!" She tripped into the bathroom and slid the tiny bold across, knowing that the flimsy door would not last two minutes if Adam wanted to get inside. She looked at the tiny window and contemplated her escape. It opened from the bottom by releasing a small catch. The glass could then be pushed outwards and secured in place with the attached hinge. Wendy realised that the possibility of squeezing herself through the small aperture without making noise and being detected was an impossibility.

"What're you doing in there?" Adam's voice did not hide his curiosity.

Wendy forced a laugh. "I'm having a wee, what do you think I'm doing, baking a cake?"

The caravan shifted and she felt him stand up. Imagining that he had his ear next to the closed bathroom door, she quickly sat on the toilet and forced herself to urinate.

Appeased, Adam moved away. He searched around her bed for her phone but failed to find it. He sat back down and waited.

Wendy delayed coming out for as long as she dared. She turned on the little tap and made a lot of noise washing her hands and pretending to look for a clean towel. She tried to find something that she could use to defend herself, but other than a small aerosol and the toilet brush, she came up empty-handed. When she felt that she could not possibly stay in there any longer without raising his suspicions, she slowly pulled the catch across and stepped into the van.

"That's better," she plastered on a smile that she hoped would be convincing and sat on the edge of her bed. "So, Adam, tell me about yourself. What's it like working for Scotland Yard? Or are you involved with Interpol?"

Adam looked at her with a vacant expression as he tried to come up with an answer. Wendy wondered how he had managed to hoodwink them all into believing he was a detective. A quick flash of a fake badge and they'd all fallen for him and his story.

Abruptly the circus site came alive with activity.

"FIRE! FIRE!"

"GET THE HOSES."

"CALL THE FIRE BRIGADE!"

Adam jumped up and opened the door. He stared out into the melange of circus artists, some in their nightwear and others half dressed as they ran helter-skelter around the site in various degrees of panic. He could see flames licking out, stretching upwards towards the night's sky.

"DON`T JUST STAND THERE! FETCH WATER!" one of the clowns shouted at Adam as he passed the caravan. "GET A BUCKET, MAN!"

"GET UP, EVERYONE GET OUT AND HELP!"

Wendy stared at Adam, his body half out of the caravan, he seemed almost frozen in time. She wondered if he was trying to decide if this was the perfect time and opportunity to commit a murder. With all the commotion outside, one-shot with the silencer and he could escape into the night before anyone realised that he had gone. Wendy shivered at the thought. She contemplated opening a window by her bed and clambering out of there, but now that the curtains were open, she had no valid reason to close them, especially with all the commotion outside. She pondered scrambling past him and making a run for it, but she doubted she'd be able to succeed.

"What's going on?"

Adam turned to face her. "There's some sort of fire over by the caravans." His eyes turned a steely black and Wendy tensed, automatically knowing what he was thinking and that her time was up. For a moment, he turned back towards the chaotic scene outside, then he seemed to make up his mind. Leaning forwards, he planned to close the door, do the dastardly deed, and make his escape. As he grabbed for the handle, Benjamín appeared out of nowhere and yanked it back open. The door's propulsion jettisoned Adam forwards. He fell out of the caravan and ran a few steps into the throng of people as he tried, unsuccessfully to regain his balance. He landed awkwardly on the ground, scuffing his knees on the hard concrete. At the same time, Wendy heard knocking on her bedroom window. It was Miguel.

"Wendy, quick! Open the window."

In seconds she had lifted the latch and pushed the window as far open as it would go.

Miguel held out his hands. "Climb out, quickly, I've got you!"

Wendy did not need telling twice. She yanked up her nightdress and clambered out. Miguel held her around the waist to steady her descent.

"Come on," he said. "Follow me!"

"What are you both still doing inside?" Benjamín said to the prone figure of Adam laying on the ground. "Come on! Everyone must help to put the fire out, or the whole bloody site will go up! We'll lose everything!"

Adam jumped up, annoyed that his master plan was going awry. "I must get Wendy," he headed towards the van.

"Man, she's out already didn't you see her go?" Benjamín pointed in the wrong direction to throw him off the scent.

Miguel bustled Wendy around the outskirts of the site and headed towards the safety of Edwaldo's trailer.

Adam tried to pinpoint her position through the middle of the disorientated crowd. He heard sirens in the distance and assumed the fire-brigade were on their way. He set off running, constantly scanning the site for any sign of Wendy.

Unfortunately for him, by now, the story about his intentions had spread and whichever direction he tried to go, someone or something slowed his path. He was handed buckets and told to fill them, he was tripped over by extended hosepipes, he was hit over the head with a long ladder and covered in foam from a fire extinguisher. If anyone had been passing by, they would have assumed they were watching the clowns practising their slapstick act.

Now, wet-through, cut, bruised, covered in foam, and with a lump on his forehead the size of a duck egg, Adam finally stopped running. He stood in the middle of the pandemonium, his eyes were blurred and stinging from the foam, and he stopped for a moment to wipe the spume from his face with angry swipes and flicks of his hands. When he slowly opened his eyes, peering through bleared vision, he frowned in confusion. The frenetic activity all around him had morphed to a sudden stillness. The shouting had become an uneasy silence, and when his vision finally cleared, he found himself surrounded by a group of Brazilian police. A circle of circus artists stood behind them. He sagged with the realisation that he had failed. The black tendrils of smoke swirling angrily upwards from the doused fire cruelly reminded him of his unaccomplished task and the money he would never get that had also gone up in smoke.

Everyone followed the police as they handcuffed Adam and marched him towards the waiting police cars.

The girls stood huddled together, watching the scene.

"So, Lisa," Wendy said with a grin, as they watched the police car pull away. "What was that you said on the plane about circus life being a magical place with grassy fields, twinkling fairy lights and everyone lives happily ever after...?"

CHAPTER ELEVEN

SIX MONTHS LATER:

Wendy could not believe that she had flown back to Brazil and was standing at the entrance to the circus site, only in a different field. After the whole sniper affair, she had left the show as soon as possible and was not afraid to admit that she had not missed circus life. Give her a proper bed and a decent sized bathroom any day! But she would not have missed today for the world.

Unlike her arrival almost a year earlier, this time she was met with open arms. Old faces came out to say hello and wish her well. She asked for directions to Fernando's door, then knocked and waited. Sarah opened it and squealed with glee.

"Wendy! I'm so glad you came!"

"Me too," she replied. She glanced around the huge trailer and spied Fernando, all dressed up sitting in his wheelchair. "Hi there. How're you doing?"

"Not so bad, under the circumstances," he smiled. "I couldn't have coped if it wasn't for Sarah. She's my saviour."

"Ha! More like your slave!" Sarah replied playfully. "You can put your bags in here if you want, Wendy," Sarah pointed to the main bedroom. "Do you fancy a drink? You know, while you're getting changed."

"Nope, not for me, thank you. I'm teetotal now, would you believe?"

"Really? That's great."

"Yeah, once I got back home I checked myself into a clinic and I've turned my life around."

"That's fabulous news!"

Wendy heard a second knock on the trailer door and in walked Lisa and Miguel.

"Wendy!" Lisa threw herself into Wendy's arms. "I'm so pleased to see you. How're things?"

"Fantastic actually, but what about you?" Wendy stared at Lisa's flat stomach and then felt awkward to continue. Had Lisa lost the baby? Had she had a termination? Or had it come prematurely? If her memory served her well, Lisa should be in her eighth month of pregnancy.

Lisa followed Wendy's eyes and deduced what she was thinking. "Oh!" She said with relief. "Don't worry, there was never a baby."

"What? How come?"

"The pregnancy test that I took turned out to be a false positive."

"But how is that possible?"

"The test was out of date. Miguel became concerned when I didn't seem to be getting any symptoms like morning sickness, a furry tongue, hunger pangs, or weight gain so we went to see a doctor. He confirmed that I wasn't pregnant."

Wendy did not know whether to sympathise or congratulate her. "Wow! How... how did you feel?"

"Mixed emotions at first, but in the end relieved. It meant that I had no ties to Mario and I was free to pursue my life with Miguel."

"But tell her the rest of the tale," Miguel urged grinning from ear to ear.

"Oh, yeah!" Lisa giggled. "We've just found out that I'm four weeks pregnant!"

Wendy and Sarah hugged and congratulated her as Fernando shook Miguel's hand.

"Well done, mate!" He felt slightly envious that he and Sarah would never be able to have kids, but they had talked about it and Sarah was not that bothered. '

"Listen, Wendy, I don't want to rush you, but we need to be seated in the tent in half an hour. So, I think, you should start getting ready," Sarah suggested.

Wendy gave her a mock salute and ran into the bedroom.

The tent looked fabulous, the ring had been decorated with the most fragrant, beautiful flowers of every possible colour all around the ring-fences. Elegant decorations, similar to coat stands, hoisted flowering baskets of the same ringside flowers, and the altar in the middle of the ring had a small, matching sprig across the top. Fairy lights twinkled from the cupola downwards, in lines of synchronised lights that resembled a waterfall. Benjamín stood to attention, looking left and right like a nervous soldier as the first bars of the wedding march flared from the speakers. He spied Melissa walking towards him accompanied by her father. Her elegant, white dress of satin and lace, perfectly highlighted her femininity. Her hair adorned with the same flowers reminded everyone of an ephemeral being as though a fairy was in their midst. The entire proceedings seem even more magical than they actually were.

Edwaldo stood next to Benjamín and squeezed his arm. "You've got a good one there, don't ever let her go."

"I don't intend to," Benjamín replied.

Wendy, Sarah, and Lisa, dressed in elegant bridesmaids' dresses followed Melissa while she walked down the aisle.

When the ceremony began, Wendy looked around at all the familiar faces. One member of the circus was conspicuous by his absence. "Where's Mario?" she whispered to Sarah.

"He left. He couldn't stand being on the show and seeing Lisa and Miguel together."

Wendy grinned. "Good riddance to bad rubbish," she whispered.

"Hear, hear!"

The priest coughed and then continued. "And now it is the part of the ceremony where the bride and groom can say their vows. Melissa, why don't you go first?"

Holding hands and looking into his eyes, Melissa began. "From the first moment I saw you, I knew that you were special. You are wonderful, kind and you make me laugh, and I think that is an important aspect of a marriage. I promise to love you until my dying day."

When snivels and tears flowed from the majority of the captive audience, Benjamín took over.

"Melissa, as you know, our relationship hasn't always been so straightforward. you told me that you felt I was holding something back, some secret that you could never quite solve. Well, today on our wedding day, before you say 'I do', there is something that I need to confess."

There was a discernible gasp from most members of the circus congregation.

"Oh Fuck!" Lisa said quietly, expressing what Wendy and Sarah had also been thinking. They looked across at Melissa. She looked as though she were about to faint.

"What?" she croaked, fiddling with her veil and wishing it were thicker so that he couldn't see the fear in her eyes.

"Melissa, I needed to find someone who loved me for who I am. And you did just that. But the truth is, I'm not just the ringmaster and general dogsbody that I led you to believe. You see, Edwaldo is my brother. We own the circus together."

Wendy, Sarah, and Lisa looked at each other and gave a collective sigh.

"Thank God for that!" Wendy exclaimed. "I thought he was going to say he had twenty-six kids with other women or something."

The other two giggled, partly from relief.

"I've always preferred to take a back seat and let Edwaldo take the reins," Benjamín continued. "You fell in love with me believing me to be a nobody, and that's why I love you. You love me for me, not for my status or my money. I promise to love and take care of you from now until eternity. Now, Melissa, will you please be my wife?"

With tears flowing down her cheeks, Melissa nodded in acceptance and the entire congregation cheered with happiness and relief.

"Oh my God! I feel like I'm living in a fairy tale!" Lisa sniffled and wiped her eyes on a handkerchief."

Wendy grinned. "Forever the romantic!"

After the ceremony, the tent doubled as the reception venue, and when the party was in full swing, Wendy and the girls walked over to congratulate the happy couple.

Melissa hugged her with a genuine warmth that made Wendy even happier with what she was now about to do. "Here, this is your wedding gift from me."

Melissa, with Benjamín by her side, opened the envelope. When they saw the huge amount of money written on the check, Melissa's mouth dropped open. "Wendy, we can't possibly accept all this."

"Yes you can, and you will."

"But how can you possibly afford this?"

Wendy smiled. "Well to cut a rather long story short, when I flew home from here, I'd only been back at my parents' house for a couple of days when a man knocked on the door asking for me. I was petrified to tell you the truth. Not only for me but for my parents' safety too. I automatically thought he was another hitman and he had found me.

"What happened?" Lisa bit her nails, unsure that she could listen to the rest of the story.

"I phoned the police but when they arrived, the man hung around. It turned out, he was a solicitor and he'd come to inform me that my husband had died in a rather `iffy´ car crash." She held up her fingers to imitate inverted commas.

"Oh, I'm sorry!" Melissa said.

"Don't be sorry," Wendy replied. "I was glad to see the back of him! Anyway, it turned out that he hadn't only taken out insurance on me, but on himself too. In the end, the insurance company was unable to prove foul play, and they were forced to hand over millions of pounds."

Wow! That's amazing," Melissa replied. "But really," she waggled the cheque in Wendy's direction, "this is too much."

"Not at all," Wendy reach inside her clutch bag a second time and presented Sarah and Lisa with a matching cheque.

They were momentarily lost for words, then they squealed with laughter and hugged Wendy, jumping round in circles.

Sarah kissed her. "Thank you, this will help a lot to reform the trailer and make it suitable for Fernando's needs. Hell, what am I thinking of? With all this money, we can buy a new trailer, tailor-made for him!"

Then it was Lisa's turn to kiss Wendy. "Thank you so much. I can't tell you how happy I am, but I'm also really pleased to hear that you are safe from any more danger."

Wendy smiled at the people she now considered family. If it hadn't been for their forethought, she doubted she would still be alive.

"Well, Lisa, I have to admit, that it seems you were right in the end."

Lisa looked puzzled. "Right about what?"

"Well, it would appear that circus stories do have happy endings after all."

THE END

Thank you for taking the time to read 'The Circus Affair'. If you enjoyed it, please consider telling your friends as word of mouth is an author's best friend.

Please post a short review. Every single one is hugely important to budding authors. They make a difference and will be greatly appreciated. Also, don't forget to email me with your ideas in regards to the true events within this book. Send your ideas to: antologiadeaguilas@gmail.com then I can also notify you of new releases, book discounts, freebies and competitions. Thank you in advance, Michele.

Discover more books by Michele E. Northwood at https://www.nextchapter.pub/authors/michele-e-northwood

Want to know when one of our books is free or discounted? Join the newsletter at http://eepurl.com/bqqB3H

ABOUT THE AUTHOR

Michele has had an interesting life. She was a dancer, magician and fire-eater who toured the world for over twenty years in theatre, musicals and circus. When she retired from entertainment, she went back to school and now has a First Class Honours degree in Modern languages, (English and Spanish).

During her years in entertainment, she has been in the Guinness Book of Records for being part of the world's largest Human mobile while working for the Circus of Horrors as their first "Girl inside a bottle". She has rubbed shoulders with Sting, Chris de Burg, David Copperfield, Claudia Schiffer and Maurice Gibb from the Bee Gees. She has worked as a knife throwers assistant, assisted a midget in his balancing act and has also taken part in the finale of a Scorpions concert.

Michele currently lives in Spain with her Spanish husband, Randy, three dogs and two cats, and is an English teacher. She prepares students for the prestigious Cambridge English Examinations. She enjoys teaching immensely. There is a lot of laughter in her classroom and Michele feels that the children keep her young.

Michele is concerned about climate change, the abundance of plastic pollution and hates the way man-unkind treat the other species which inhabit this beautiful planet which we are slowly destroying. She loves living in the countryside with views of the sea and likes nothing better than to sit on the terrace at the end of the day, look up at the stars and contemplate.

The author's first book, "Fishnets in the Far East: A dancer's diary in Korea", is now a double Award Winner! It won Best Memoir 2019 with The Reader's Choice Awards and was a Finalist in the Book Excellence Awards 2020. The sequel, (but also a stand-alone novel), "Fishnets and Fire-eating: A Dancer's true story in Japan" is due to be released soon, and she is currently working on a paranormal, horror thriller.

The author can be contacted/followed at:
https://www.facebook.com/michele.e.northwoodauthor
https://twitter.com/northwood_e
https://www.pinterest.es/nextchapterpub/pinterest-board-michele-e-northwood/fishnets-in-the-far-east-a-dancer-s-diary-in-korea/

OTHER BOOKS BY THE AUTHOR:

Fishnets in the Far East: A Dancer's Diary in Korea (A true story)
Fishnets and Fire-eating: A Dancer's True story in Japan
The Spanish Retreat
The Circus Affair